"TEN NIGHTMARES YOU'LL NEVER FORGET"
—Chicago Tribune

"Reminds us unforgettably of what was happening in the blazing ruin of Hitler's Third Reich" —The New York Times

"Ingenious" —Springfield Republican

"Drives home the horror of Nazi atrocities"
—Baltimore Sun

"Excellent, fascinating, shocking" —Tulsa World

"Some of the most spine-chilling things to hit print in a long time" —Dallas Times-Herald

"Provocative" —Atlanta Constitution

"Extraordinary" —Miami Herald

THE NIGHTMARE

C. S. FORESTER

A DELL BOOK

Published by
DELL PUBLISHING CO., INC.
750 Third Avenue
New York 17, N.Y.

Reprinted by arrangement with
Little, Brown and Company
Boston, Mass.

First Dell printing—October, 1961

Printed in U.S.A.

INTRODUCTION

Not one of these stories tells of an actual happening, but all of them except the last could easily have happened. From the thousands of pages of matter—sworn evidence at the Nuremberg and Belsen trials, sober history, self-exculpatory memoirs, and actual documents, which have appeared since the fall of the Nazi regime—could be gathered material for many stories, most of them hardly credible on account of their cynicism or horror. There is Naukocks's affidavit regarding the "criminals" left dead beside the Gleiwitz radio station; the evidence against Hartjenstein in the Natzweiler trial, and that against Kramer in the Belsen trial; from these sources came, as will be obvious, suggestions for some of the stories in this book. But those sources are not easily accessible and to some extent are tedious reading, so that it is hard for the average reader to become acquainted with the remarkable possibilities of unfettered power. During the dozen years of the Nazi regime in Germany things happened that could hardly find a parallel in the most debased days of the Roman Empire; crimes were committed—usually quite legally, according to the letter of the law of the land—which make those of

Jack the Ripper and Landru appear quite insignificant. A fantastic pyramid of a new governing class arose, mortared with blood although honeycombed by suspicion, and only eventually undermined by military failure. A few more victories in Russia, or a moment of irresolution on the part of the British people, and that regime might be in existence to this day; it is less than twenty years ago since it fell, although that seems hard to believe. Less than twenty years ago people were dying by the hundred thousand at the word of one man, and that man not quite sane. It happened twenty years ago; it seems quite certain that similar things are happening at this very moment in other countries where ruling gangs are established in power. There is no purpose in studying history unless the lessons of the past are to influence policy in the present, and present policy can only have a basis in the lessons of the past.

CONTENTS

EVIDENCE

It was towards the end of Otto Sasse's third year in a concentration camp that he won his release. He went in when he was seventeen and he came out at twenty. Because he did not die under the treatment he recieved, nor break down under the labor he had to perform, he had grown very hard and tough. He was lean, yet covered with muscle, his hands were horny, and he could do physical work for fourteen hours a day without over-much exhaustion; he did that every day during the summer of 1939, often waist-deep in water, while he was employed on the construction of the great bridge across the Oder.

Those three years had been a time of triumph for Germany, marked by the absorption of Austria and Czechoslovakia and Memel, the humiliation of England and France, and the snubbing of the President of the United States. News of these great events had penetrated into the concentration camp; indeed it was proclaimed aloud in them, not only by loud-speakers blaring out the speeches of the Fuehrer, but also by the talks given by Party indoctrination officers. For the Party in those years seemed to adopt a double attitude towards its political prisoners. It killed them quickly or slowly, but at the same time it endeavored to convert them to the Party doctrines, acting almost as if it believed men had souls to save and wished them to die cherishing orthodox beliefs.

So that as the summer progressed Sasse had some knowledge of the new crisis in which the Reich was involved. He knew about the demand for the return of Danzig to the Reich, and about the related demand regarding the Corridor. Even in the speeches of the Fuehrer and in the lectures by the indoctrination officers he was aware of an increasing tension, of an excitement more heightened even than that over the Czech crisis. He could tell there was a great danger of war; the possibility was obvious that Germany might soon be exposed to an assault by the other powers of Europe, and his feelings regarding it were turbulent and harassing to him.

The crime that had brought him into the concentration camp, a month before he had been due to enter a youth camp, was one of omission. He had neglected to betray his own father. In very truth he had known nothing of his father's activities; he had not even suspected them until the night when the police came bursting into the house, hauling from their beds all the people there and placing them under arrest. But Wilhelm Sasse was not there, as the exasperated police discovered after searching everywhere. He may have been forewarned; it may have been pure chance, but he had not returned that night, and now there was no possibility of his returning. He had disappeared into the German underworld, and it would be largely a matter of chance if he were ever arrested.

Wilhelm Sasse the father had been engaged in a conspiracy against the Reich; there were a thousand arrests in Berlin that night, mostly of men who had been petty officials of trades unions before the Party came into power. These misguided men had been ungrateful enough to the Fuehrer, and blind enough to the benefits he had conferred on the Reich, to be discontented with the new state of affairs. On the other hand they had also been too blind to detect the presence of Party agents in their midst, with the result that well-organized simultaneous raids had effected the arrest of nearly all of them; only a few ringleaders escaped.

Aged seventeen, Otto Sasse the son had been let off lightly; the questioning to which he had been submitted was searching but was not severe—he did not know about the way his mother was questioned—and the results left the questioners convinced he had no knowledge at all of his father's present whereabouts. But he had been a member of a household whose head was guilty of the blackest treason, and confinement in a concentration camp was clearly indicated for him. Nor could there be any chance of liberty for a man whose father was hiding in the underworld conspiring against the Fuehrer and the Reich. Young Sasse had been nearly three years in prison by the summer of 1939; three years in which to grow from a boy to a young man—three years of confinement.

There was an unusual parade one afternoon at the camp. An unknown officer in an S.A. uniform walked down the lines making a selection, a youngish man, not yet thirty, and spectacled, and a little stoop-shouldered. He looked out of place in his uniform, as if he were a poet, unbelievable as it might be that that sort of poet should have high rank in the Party. And he was accompanied by a sergeant, also young, in a uniform unknown to Sasse, field gray with black epaulets. Black was the color of the SS, the dreaded color, and when the sergeant came down the line along with the spectacled officer it could be seen that his badges bore the SS in Gothic characters. Young Sasse guessed he must be a member of the Waffen SS, the private field army that had been built up during the last few years to supplement—and keep in hand—the regular army of the Reich. The sergeant bore himself with all the pride and swagger to be expected of a sergeant in a corps d'élite.

Sasse had attended many selection parades, most of them ending in slaughter, but this was different. The young officer selected only thirty men, and these were all men in their twenties, active and vigorous, and Sasse was among them. He stole cautious glances at his neighbors. No one ever knew what might happen next in a prison camp. No one could ever guess, for things went on in a prison camp that no imagination could conceive. If one wished to stay alive in a prison camp one had to be quick-witted and ruthless, and Sasse prepared himself.

At a command from the sergeant the thirty men formed up and marched briskly off the parade ground. A further order from the sergeant wheeled them round. They were not heading for the main gate.

"What's the new idea?" whispered the man next to Sasse, but no one could answer him.

They marched to the side gate, the one which was never used, but this time it was open, and through it

they went, into the barracks of the SS who supplied the
guards for the camp. A few guards off duty—Sasse knew
most of them by sight—looked at them with curiosity,
and Sasse looked back at them. They were curious at this
sight of prisoners in their hideous uniforms marching in,
but Sasse could read no more than curiosity in their
faces. Whatever fate awaited the prisoners, it did not
appear as if the guards were in on the secret. And at this
new experience, at marching into sacred ground where
they had never set foot before, the prisoners could not
restrain themselves, and broke into a buzz of chatter, but
the next order from the sergeant silenced it, and the
order that followed wheeled them round again to the
door of a barracks hut outside which stood a party of
men in the Waffen SS uniforms.

"March in!" ordered the sergeant. "One man by each
bed."

It was a spotless clean barracks room, with beds
spaced at regular intervals down each side and beside
each bed were the hooks and the lockers for military
equipment. The men filed in and took their places; those
of them who had experienced military service set the
example to the other of standing at the end of the beds.
The sergeant and the officer followed them in, and the
door was shut. The pair exchanged a few words and the
spectacled officer stepped forward to where they could
all see him.

"*Achtung!*" barked the sergeant, and the officer began
to speak while the prisoners stood to attention.

"This is your great opportunity, men," said the officer; his voice was beautifully modulated, not persuasive
so much as convincing. "War threatens. The Reich is in

peril, as you know. Jewish capitalism menaces our existence. The armies of the Western Powers are mobilizing
on our frontiers, determined on perpetuating the wrongs
inflicted on our country. But we shall strike them down,
as our Fuehrer has promised."

He paused; so far he had said almost nothing that the
prisoners had not heard already, but he had said it well,
with conviction. Then he went on.

"As I said, this is your great opportunity. A deed call-
ing for great daring and devotion has been planned
which a few brave men can carry out. You have been
selected for it. For the Fatherland! For the Reich! An
hour of peril, an hour of exertion, and you will have
struck a blow that will be remembered through history.
And then you will be citizens again. Never again will
you be inside barbed wire. You will be free, restored to
every right and privilege enjoyed by members of the
master race to which you belong. Those shameful clothes
that you wear now you will never see again; you will be
soldiers wearing the honorable uniform of the armed
forces, entitled to the comradeship and the dignity that
uniform confers. Men, I know that you will all go willingly into this great adventure."

He paused again. His face was alight with enthusiasm;
he looked like a man inspired. Sasse had listened to him
with the idealism of twenty years old, and with the cynicism of a man who had spent three years in a concentration camp. Danger? Death? They seemed likely enough
in this unknown adventure. And yet on the other hand
there was the promise of freedom, of an end to imprisonment, the filthiness and shame of life in prison huts. And
Sasse was only twenty. His country was in danger even

though it was the country whose rulers sought his father's life and kept him behind barbed wire. For three years, since he was seventeen, he had heard no news except what was broadcast from loud-speakers and what had been told him by indoctrination officers. Maybe propaganda had worked on him in the absence of any counteracting influence. Maybe he felt that his fatherland was threatened by unscrupulous foreign powers who envied and feared the strength that the new regime had built up in Germany. Maybe the simple German patriotism that his father had felt and had instilled in his son had been reorientated; maybe it still existed pure. Otto was ready to strike a blow for his country. He was ready to die for it, as well as being ready to risk death in exchange for freedom. The officer caught his eye, and noticed how the boy's face reflected his own enthusiasm, and he smiled at him.

"There is no need for me to say more," he said. "One day—two days—a week from now at most and we shall start on our adventure. I shall be with you; that is why I say 'we.' Until then obey your sergeant. He will look after you."

The officer turned away and the sergeant opened the door for him, saluting as he passed out into the August sunshine. Now it was the sergeant's turn to speak.

"Well, my lucky lads," he said, "now you're here and you'd better make the best of it. Give me no trouble and I'll give you none. No talking after lights out, keep your barracks clean, and I'll ask no more of you. But the man who causes trouble—back he goes in *there* with a note to the commandant."

The sergeant's thumb jerked back over his shoulder

towards the concentration camp to indicate what he meant by "in there."

"How long are we going to be here, Sergeant?" asked a voice.

"Perhaps a day. Perhaps a month," said the sergeant. "No one knows. You will draw your uniforms this afternoon."

"What uniforms, Sergeant?"

"Now, that's enough questions. You'll get them this afternoon, I said."

And when the uniforms were served out the men were not much wiser. Each man received a neat khaki uniform like nothing any of them had seen before, not even in such a multiuniformed country as Germany. The cap badges and insignia meant nothing to any of them, however much they puzzled over them when they were back in their barracks room. The sergeant had taken some care to see that each man was properly fitted. He issued each man a shirt and a set of underclothing, and a pair of good boots.

"Now get the lice scrubbed off you before you change," he ordered. He was a jovial man, by no means severe. "I'll inspect you in an hour's time. Each man must be properly dressed by then."

In the barracks room a cautious argument began about the clothing; cautious, because the inmates had been drawn from all quarters of the concentration camp and did not know each other, and everyone feared the presence of an informer.

"It's a Polish uniform," declared one.

"Polish be damned," said another. "What would we need Polish uniforms for?"

Sasse fingered his uniform and could only wonder. Meanwhile there was luxury in which to revel, shower baths and hot water and plenty of soap, clean under-clothing to put on, the hideous camp clothing to be discarded—forever, the spectacled Nazi officer had promised. In the late afternoon sunshine they formed up outside the barracks door while the sergeant in-spected them keenly. He looked every man over, up and down, front and back.

"That coat's a bad fit," he said to one man. "Report for another."

None of the clothing the men wore was new, but it was all clean and not badly worn. And the solid feeling of good boots on the feet was remarkably pleasant. Even more pleasant was the supper they were served, food and coffee such as not one of them had tasted since his arrest.

"SS rations, by God!" said one man, smacking his lips.

By the time lights out came a certain community of feeling had already grown up among the thirty young men who had been gathered together for the unknown adventure. Talk grew a little more free—in fact it called for a sharp order from the sergeant to bring it to an end. It was a sweltering hot night, it being the end of August, and the barracks room was overheated by the sun that had blazed on it all day. Sasse turned over in his bed— a strangely comfortable bed—several times before he went to sleep.

Next morning there was an excellent breakfast, with each man eying his companions, strange in their uni-forms in the morning light again. Half a dozen cheap razors had been served out to them, so that each man was cleanly shaved, waiting in turn to use them, while reveling again in the shower baths and the almost sufficient and spotless latrine accommodation.

"Now for the rest of your equipment," said the sergeant after breakfast.

It was the sort of thing any soldier might expect to have issued to him: pack and ammunition pouches, water bottle and bayonet on webbing straps. But it was not German army equipment, as the men who had done their military service showed by the curiosity with which they handled it. The steel helmets were different from any Sasse remembered having seen in pictures. Pack and pouches were full and heavy.

"Keep your hands off that!" snapped the sergeant at the men who began to open the pouches. "And I'll tell you now, in case you start having ideas, that those cartridges are empty. There's no explosive in them. Now put that gear on and I'll see if it fits."

Each man put his arms through the straps, buckled the belts, and felt the weight of the equipment on his shoulders, while the sergeant examined each man, and saw that the equipment was properly adjusted, and the helmets properly put on. He was again very painstaking about it.

"All right," decided the sergeant at last. "Now I want each man to hang his equipment here. Remember the number of your hook, so that you can find your own quickly."

"Here" was not in their barracks room, but in the building where the equipment had been served out, and beneath each hook stood a rifle. The sergeant marched them back to their own barracks.

"Dismiss!" he ordered.

That was strangest of all, the sensation of being idle, of having nothing to do. The men had slaved twelve or fifteen hours a day ever since their arrest, and now it was unnatural to them not to be occupied and not to be dog tired. Talk among them began slowly, but it soon grew louder and more animated as arguments developed on the insoluble question of their destiny.

"Prisoners of war! That's what we'll be," declared one man.

A big man with a scar on his face announced his contempt for the suggestion in the brief and filthy words of the camp.

"What prisoners?" asked another man. "Whose prisoners?"

"Poles, perhaps," said the first man. "You said these were Polish uniforms."

"Polish rubbish!" said someone else.

"Well, we are going to fight the Poles, aren't we?" persisted the first speaker. "Remember that broadcast—?"

"I think these are Bulgarian uniforms," announced someone else.

It was a new suggestion which called for fresh debate. Many of the men were a little vague about where Bulgaria was and what was its political alignment. Then someone else came in with a new remark.

"That Nazi officer with the spectacles said there'd be danger in it," he said.

That called for a moment of silence. It was a *memento mori* to these men; they had left the shadow of the gas chamber behind them and had felt momentarily immortal.

"Hell!" said the man with the scar. "What's danger to *us?*"

"He didn't give us any choice," someone else pointed out. "He didn't ask us if we'd volunteer."

"Hell!" repeated the man with the scar. "Who wouldn't have volunteered when we were—in there? I know I would have."

"But perhaps they'll want—" began another, and then the sentence died on his lips and he looked guiltily about him in terror lest anyone should have guessed how he had intended to end it. He had been going to suggest that "they" were going to force them to do something in support of the regime which might go against the conscience of the inmates, and that would have been a highly dangerous thing to say if there were an informer present.

"Who cares what they want?" said the man with the scar. "I'll do it. And—"

The man with the scar broke off his sentence too. He had been going to say that he intended to take good care that he would come through alive, at whatever price to anyone else, but he had seen in time that it would not be policy to give warning of it. But the others had guessed and glances were interchanged. There was another moment of silence as everyone digested the information about the man with the scar even though it was information that everyone would, after almost no thought, have taken for granted regarding anyone from the camp who was a stranger to them.

"What are those rifles for if the ammunition is no good?" asked someone, changing the subject.

There was plenty to talk about all morning, and then

there was a dinner with food of such quality and in such quantity that they were all impressed, and they could doze and lounge about all the afternoon while waiting for the next meal. As early as the third morning the sergeant could comment on their appearance.

"You're fattening up now, lads," he said.

It was true. A few days of idleness and plenty of good food had begun to turn them from hollow-cheeked skeletons to burly men. And, at the same time, the quarrels began, as was to be expected among men who had nothing to do. The sergeant heard the din and came in and quelled them.

"Very well, then," said the sergeant. "If you can't keep yourselves out of mischief I must do it for you. The square for you, my boys. I'll keep you busy."

So he did; he had them out in the parade yard for hours at a time giving them close-order drill, marching, wheeling, forming column and then line, until they were dismissed to their barracks room healthily tired and less likely to quarrel. On the night after the second day of drill there was a sudden alarm. The barracks door was flung open and the lights switched on.

"Turn out! Turn out!" bellowed the sergeant. "Five minutes to dress! Don't shave."

He himself had plainly hurried into his uniform. The men dressed quickly and formed up under the light outside the barracks.

"Right turn. Quick march. File in there and draw your rifles and equipment."

He went round each man to see he had his equipment properly put on.

"Here," said the sergeant. He unlocked a safe that

stood against the wall and took out from it a small pile of pocketbooks and papers. "One of each kind to each of you. Put the book in your right-hand breast pocket and the letters in the other and don't look at them. D'you hear me, Sasse? Don't look at them, I said. Now fall in again outside."

He marched them in the darkness to where stood three motor trucks in column and he herded them into the middle one, climbing after them and seating himself at the tailboard. The motors roared and off went the trucks into darkness out through the gates and into the dark countryside.

"Sergeant," said a voice in the darkness, "where are we going?"

"Shut your mouth," snapped the sergeant.

They sat swaying in the truck as it thundered along the road. They bumped against each other, encumbered with their equipment. Even their helmets bumped together sometimes, painfully. Suddenly a bright ray of light stabbed along the interior of the truck. The sergeant had switched on an electric torch and by its diffused light they could just make out his dark figure behind it and the automatic pistol in his hand.

"You, Kessel," he snapped, "I heard you. Put that bayonet back."

They heard the weapon returned to its sheath.

"It's no use, boys," went on the sergeant. "There's twenty SS in the truck ahead, and twenty in the truck behind, with machine guns. Lift a finger and you're dead, all of you."

The truck rumbled on in silence for hours, lurching and swaying. Suddenly there was a halt, and voices. A light shone in at the rear of the truck. They saw an officer, in field gray, helmeted and in full equipment.

"Orders for you, Sergeant," said the officer.

"My orders come direct from the ministry, sir," said the sergeant.

"These are from the ministry. They were telephoned along the route tö stop you."

The officer handed the slip to the sergeant, who read it by the light of his torch.

"Sign for it," said the officer, and the sergeant signed. "You can turn at the crossroad here."

"Thank you, sir," said the sergeant.

The trucks reversed themselves in the road, and started to rumble back in the direction whence they had come.

"Home again, boys," said the sergeant.

"What's going on, Sergeant?"

"I wish I knew."

Dawn was already breaking. They could look out across the flat North German plain, across the stubble fields where the rye had just been harvested, at the occasional cattle and horses, and they could see more than that. In the fields off the road there were camps without number, bivouacs, immense parks of tanks and motor transport, bursting into activity again with the coming of day. There were military police at the crossroads and field gray uniforms everywhere. The *Wehrmacht* was moving up for the kill, and to the prisoners so long confined it was a rare treat to see the outside world again, and a world so full of activity at that. They chattered like schoolboys, peering out past the sergeant. Then they swung in again at the gate of the SS barracks and halted.

"Return your rifles and equipment, your books and your papers," ordered the sergeant; and when that was done—"I'll see there's breakfast for you."

Now there was more to argue about than ever. The men debated the strange events of the night, trying to correlate them with their other experiences.

"What were those papers?" asked one.

"Pay books, of course," answered someone else.

"There were letters with mine," said someone. "Old letters."

"Did you read them?"

"Didn't get a chance."

"Nor did I."

The sergeant had them out again for close-order drill, and after their disturbed night and the heavy exercise they slept soundly as soon as the lights were out. Yet once more their sleep was broken; the events of the previous night began to repeat themselves. The sergeant woke them as before; once again they donned uniform and equipment and helmets, put their books and papers in their pockets, and hurried with their rifles into the waiting truck. Once again they lurched and rumbled along the dark road. But this time they were not turned back. Daylight found them still heading eastward; it was only just light enough to see when the trucks drew up. The sergeant scrambled out.

"Down you come, boys," he ordered.

They were cold and stupid, and stood in a huddled mass until the sergeant formed them up. Over in the east the dawn was spreading gloriously over the sky.

"Now move to it, men," snapped the sergeant. There

was a new note of asperity, of anxiety, in his voice, and
his hand rested on his belt convenient to his pistol.

It was an undistinguished part of the North German
plain in which they had halted. A mile away in the mist
of morning could be seen a church tower and indications
of a small town. Much nearer, in line with it, stood three
towering radio masts with low buildings clustering
around them. The trucks were halted on a minor, sandy
road that ran from the main road to the radio station. It
was less than half a mile long and they were half way
along it. The sergeant waved to the first truck, which
went lumbering on down the road. The third truck
was halted about thirty feet behind them. The black-
uniformed SS there were setting up a couple of machine
guns on the low bank beside the road, where they could
sweep the road and the low stubble fields beyond. Under
the menace of those guns the men were helpless. The
sergeant struggled with his anxiety and composed himself.

"We attack that radio station," he said, pointing, and
then, after a moment's hesitation, "It's all right, boys.
It's one of ours. That truck in front has a motion-picture
camera to take a film of our attack. So it has to look like
the real thing. Let's get you lined up."

The prisoners were surly and suspicious, all the same,
and the sergeant had to snap at them.

"Fix those bayonets!" he ordered. "You there, all this
half of you, get out into the field, this side. You others,
get into the field, the other side. Spread out and face
these towers. Stay up on the bank, you."

This last order was directed at Sasse, who obediently

stood in the middle of the straggling line that was forming, helmeted, equipped, with bayonets fixed.

"Now when I blow this whistle," said the sergeant,
"you all charge forward. Yell as much as you like.
Spread out farther. Farther still!"

He had to raise his voice now to a shout to reach the
men who were at the ends of the line. He stood on the
bank twenty yards behind Sasse, whistle in hand, looking over the completed arrangements.

"Now charge!" he yelled.

He blew loudly on his whistle and stepped down into
the ditch. Some of them obediently began to charge forward, one or two of them even raising a shout. A few,
still bewildered, stood where they were, holding their
rifles and looking about them; Sasse was one of these.
But it did not matter whether they stood or they
charged; they met the same fate. From ahead of them
came a sudden vicious rattle of machine guns, mowing
them down. Three bullets hit Sasse in the chest, tossing
him over lifeless into the field, and that was the end of
his doubts and wondering. The others died as the guns
traversed their fire upon them. One or two turned and
tried to run, but the guns in the rear opened fire, too,
and then ceased.

The sergeant walked back to the guns in the rear; a
corporal there was still looking along the sights.

"That one there's shamming," said the corporal, and
fired four shots. Farther along a wounded man rolled
over, and the corporal fired four more.

"See that they are all dead," said the sergeant,
hoarsely.

A car was racing along the road from Berlin; it could race in consequence of the pennon that it flew, which demanded highest priority at every crossroad. Columns of tanks and even fleets of headquarters' cars had to give way to it. Beside the chauffeur there were four men sitting in it. One was an American, one was a Spaniard, one was a Swede, and one was a German; this last was a spectacled officer of the SA.

"I'll believe it when I see it," said the American, more to himself than to the Swede and the Spaniard between whom he sat.

"It hardly seems possible," said the Swede.

"But these Poles—" said the Spaniard, with a gesture indicating that anything was possible with Poles.

The German leaned back from the front seat to join in the conversation.

"We do not know as yet," he said in his precise English, "if this dastardly attack was part of a widely spread plan. I telephoned you the moment the report reached me."

He was proud of the word "dastardly." He had found it in the dictionary during the anxious hours of the preceding evening, rehearsing to himself the phrases he would use.

"Maybe it is," said the American, with a peculiar intonation in his voice, which alarmed the German.

The latter went hurriedly in his mind through the orders he had given. If they had not been exactly carried out the consequences would be serious; very serious. The German was very conscious of the abyss that lay open at his feet. If one tiny detail were wrong, so as to reveal the attempt to hoodwink the press of the world, he was a lost man. Every hostile newspaper in the world would proclaim it, and the undoubted purity of German motives would be seriously impugned. It would be worse, far worse, than if the attempt had never been made, and he would be a dead man, or worse, far worse than dead. The minister himself had entrusted this business to him, his first job of primary importance, and the minister did not tolerate inefficiency. And it was absolutely certain that the Fuehrer himself would know about it. The spectacled officer felt chills flowing along his spine. But he was a young man of resolution as well as of imagination, and he did not allow himself to quaver—he was sufficiently warned by the note of irony in the American's voice.

"I gave orders immediately that nothing was to be touched until we arrive," he said.

"*You* gave orders?" asked the American, sharply, and the German saw the trap.

"Yes," he said, and restrained himself from being too glib, speaking as if in patient explanation. "I was the officer in charge at the office when the news arrived. So I was able, in the minister's name, to telephone at once to army headquarters and ask for full powers to deal with the situation. They were granted me, naturally."

"Naturally," said the American.

"It was six-fifteen when you telephoned me," said the Swede, looking at his notes.

There was a pause for a few seconds while all of them —the German included—made calculations.

"I suppose it's possible," conceded the American, grudgingly.

"Of course," said the German, with every appearance
of simple innocence that he could muster. It had been a
narrow escape.

"How long before we get there?" asked the American,
and the German looked at his watch.

"Three hours more at this speed," he said. "Less if we
eat our lunch as we go along."

"I vote we do," said the American to his colleagues,
and they agreed.

It was uncomfortable in that crowded car to unpack
and eat the lunch that the ministry had provided. The
champagne spilled over the carpeted floor and filled the
car with the smell of wine. They had to tear the roast
chicken to pieces with their fingers and gnaw on the
bones. But they saved time that way, while the car
whirled along beside long columns of field-gray infantry
plodding along the road.

"It looks like war, sure enough," said the American to
himself at sight of them.

"We can't be far away now," said the German, forcing
himself to look out at the countryside as if he had never
seen it before. They went over a low rise.

"There are the radio towers, sir," said the chauffeur in
German, pointing forward.

"Then it must be just here," said the spectacled officer. "It must be up this side road. Stop."

It was a short minor road, leading to the radio station;
a guard of SS men stood halfway along it, having risen
to their feet at the sight of the pennon on the car as it
drew up. The spectacled officer got down and returned
the sergeant's salute, and hastened to open the door for
the three journalists. They stood beside the car and sur-

veyed the scene. Years of disillusioning experience in Germany had taught the American not to leap hastily to conclusions. He moved forward onto the low bank and stopped again. Almost at his feet lay a dead man in uniform, beside him a rifle with fixed bayonet. Dotted here and there over the fields on either side of the road were other corpses. He counted carefully. There were thirty dead. Over there were the towers of the radio station. It seemed convincing enough.

"They tried to surprise the place at dawn, as I told you," said the spectacled officer. "They left their transport on the main road and tried to creep up to it. Fortunately it was guarded and the sentries were on the alert. You can see just how it happened."

The American looked down at the dead Otto Sasse, whose grey eyes looked past him at the sky. The pool of blood around him had dried on the parched earth, but there were still signs of it on the stubble. Those were bullet holes in the breast of the tunic, undoubtedly—this was no corpse dressed after death for the occasion. He bent down and examined the badges.

"That's a Polish uniform all right," he said to the Swede beside him. He wiped his forehead with his handkerchief, for the sun was blazing down upon him.

"Please," said the German officer, "make any examination you think necessary."

The American overcame his distaste at the thought of handling the dead. He had a duty not only to his employers but to himself and to the whole waiting world. He stooped and unbuttoned the breast pocket of the tunic, stiff with dried blood. He brought out from it a dog-eared little book, the lower edge clipped by a bullet.

There was dried blood on the book, but the print on the cover and some of the handwriting inside were legible. The Spaniard and the Swede studied it with him.

"A Polish pay book," said the American.

The German officer held out his hand for it, and turned the pages curiously, as if it was the first he ever had seen.

"I do not know much Polish," he said, "but it seems to me as if the last—what is the word?"

"Entry?" suggested the American.

"Thank you. As if the last entry was August 27. See."

The three journalists knew no Polish, but they could read the figure.

"Ye-e-es," said the American, meditatively.

He undid the other breast pocket and brought out some stained letters. No doubt about their being written in Polish.

"A woman's writing," said the Spaniard. "His mother, perhaps."

"Yes," said the American again.

He went on staring down at the dead body of Sasse. He was not going to accept the first sample the Nazis offered him. He walked out on the stubble field, looking at each corpse in turn; they were dead for sure, each one killed by machine gun or rifle bullets. This one looked as if he had been shot in the back; there was nothing deeply suspicious about that, nevertheless. He might have been killed while running away or perhaps what was visible was the exit wound of the bullet. One of the corpses farthest from the road was of a bigger man with an old scar on his face; the scar was a livid white against tanned skin which in turn had no color behind it. The American did not like doing what he had to do, but it was professional duty. The dead man lay on his back, inclining slightly to one side, one arm across his breast. The American lifted the arm; rigor had fully set in. He remembered what he had learned as a reporter dealing with homicide cases in New York; it was confirmation of the time of death as told to him. And there was no doubt that these men had died where they had fallen; the blood stains and the absence of any wheel tracks in the stubble proved that they had not been brought here dead and dumped about the field. There were cartridges in the pouches. He opened the pockets; as before, a pay book and letters, Polish letters. Holding them in his hand, he looked back to the road; the spectacled officer was in conversation with the Spaniard and paying no attention, displaying no anxiety to come and oversee his movements, neither attempting to coach him as to what he should see nor heading him off from what he should not see.

The Swede was plodding across the field towards him, and he pointed out all he had observed.

"It seems true, does it not?" said the Swede.

"I am afraid it does," said the American, and they went back to the road.

"You are satisfied now, gentlemen?" asked the spectacled officer.

The American waited for the others to nod before he agreed. He did not take his eyes from the German's face. It showed satisfaction, but not over much. No sign of relief beyond what might be expected.

"It is a most remarkable incident I agree, gentlemen," said the German, "but it proves what hot-headed people

these Poles are, and what unpleasant neighbors they
have always been to the Reich. You understand better
now how the existence of the Corridor is quite intoler-
able to the German people."

"Exactly," said the Spaniard.

"Maybe," said the American.

"At least I have your authority to say that you believe
Polish troops attempted to seize the radio station?"
asked the German. "Or is there any further examination
you would like to make?"

He looked at each in turn, and when they still hesitated he went on.

"The intelligence officer is here; he is most anxious
to commence the identification of the dead, as you can
understand, gentlemen. Headquarters are telephoning
every few minutes to ask about it. He has not been allowed to touch them so far. And there is the question of
burial."

"Oh, let him get to work," said the American.

"Thank you, gentlemen. And now you do not believe
that we Nazis tell lies all the time?"

"You tell the truth when it suits you," said the American, bitterly; and the spectacled officer bowed, control-
ling his temper.

"I expect you will want to file your stories as quickly
as possible," he said. "My car is at your disposal, gentlemen."

"You are not coming back with us?" asked the Swede.

"I shall not be able to return until much later," said
the German. "I shall have to spend much time on the
telephone, and I must begin at once—you can understand that, gentlemen. I shall be an hour or two. But

please take my car. I can find other means to return to Berlin."

The spectacled officer watched the car drive away. Not until it had turned into the main road did he allow himself to relax. He was very weary. It had been a great strain to maintain his pose under that acute observation. But it was done. Now he could telephone the news of his complete success to the minister, who would doubtless listen in person to the whole story. It would mean a decoration, promotion, congratulations. He turned and hastened towards the radio station. He must not wait a moment longer. The Fuehrer himself was waiting for his report—the Fuehrer himself! The speech the Fuehrer was to broadcast tonight could not be composed until he knew what had happened.

That was how it came about that Hitler, broadcasting to a hesitant world on the eve of the outbreak of war, was able to say that that very morning a Polish force raiding over the border had tried to seize the broadcasting station and had been repulsed with loss. Representatives of the American, Spanish, and Swedish press could bear witness to the story. That was how the spectacled officer won his promotion, and that was how Otto Sasse died.

THE BOWER OF ROSES

On the Night of the Long Knives three men drove out to the Bower of Roses. One of them was Adolph Spiegel, and he was sick with fear. His right hand rested on his coat pocket on the butt of an automatic pistol, and to his hand the unaccustomed weapon seemed incredibly large and heavy. He was sweating, and his sweat felt cold on his skin. Tonight he was seizing his one great opportunity. He was on his way to kill Lucas. Lucas was the terrible, awe-inspiring, utterly ruthless head of the Seventh Bureau in which Spiegel, in those early days of the Nazi power, had unexpectedly found himself head of a section. Lucas had never concealed his opinion of Spiegel, had called him to his face timid and cautious and unworthy to serve the Fuehrer, had mocked at his anxiety not to risk physical danger, had laughed at the mincing precision of his manner, but had retained him in his employment because he knew Spiegel to be a conscientious hard worker. Spiegel had no illusions about that; he knew that while Lucas lived he would never have much opportunity for promotion although he could be sure of having responsible and difficult work heaped on him to the limit of his endurance. But if Lucas were to die—! This was the Night of the Long Knives, and Spiegel knew that many men were dying at that very moment.

The Fuehrer was asserting his authority. Some of those who had helped him to power were asking too much of him by way of reward; some were desirous of pushing him too far and too fast along the road he had mapped for himself; some might even be suspected of something far worse, of plotting to seize some of the power that was rightfully the Fuehrer's. These men must all die, that was a matter of course; there could be no room for them in the Reich along with the Fuehrer. And when so many people were dying, another death might not be inquired into too strictly; if Lucas were killed by his trusted subordinate, and that subordinate maintained later that he had indisputable proof—nothing written, of course—that Lucas had been involved with the plotters, then his reward would be great. Probably he would be head of the department, wielding Lucas's power, enjoying Lucas's prestige. Spiegel could thrill to the thought, for the little man, although he could be sick with fear, was consumed with ambition; although he was running with cold sweat at this moment he still had his clarity of vision and his remarkable capacity for summing up motives and prejudices. On the morning after the Night of the Long Knives Lucas's death would be looked upon as the clearest proof of Lucas's guilt. The cold heavy pistol in Spiegel's pocket was the key that would open for him the door to power—the door which otherwise would always remain closed to him.

"Drive faster," he said to Klein, as though he had been used to riding in cars all his life, although the occasions when he had could be counted on ten fingers, and of course he could not drive one, which was partly why he had associated Klein and Kramer with him on this enterprise.

"I am driving as fast as I can," answered Klein. The car was rocking along the narrow road through the summer evening.

"We'll be soon enough for Lucas," said Kramer, sitting beside Klein.

Men and women working in the fields looked at the black car flashing along the road, and at the uniforms worn by the occupants. They had seen many such during the last year or two, heading for the Rosenbau—the Bower of Roses—where Lucas lived. Even in this short time since the Nazis had come to power Lucas had taken for himself a country house and estate, where he lived the life of a nobleman, copying his superiors in the party. The fat war profiteer who had previously owned the place had given it its name, and Lucas had seen no reason to change it. Perhaps it was not entirely coincidence that he was here on the Night of the Long Knives instead of being at his desk in Berlin. Lucas may have guessed what was going to happen—although very few people did—and he may have decided that out here, nineteen miles from Berlin, he would not have to declare which side he was on until the next morning, when it would be easier to pick the winner. Spiegel touched his pistol again. He knew quite well who was going to be victorious, and he was going to be on the winning side, even though the thought of the risk he was taking made his hand tremble.

They whirled through the pine woods at the end of

the lake and shot out again into the late sunshine beyond. There was the wall and the gate. Klein swung the car through, turning the corner so closely that a twig on a low tree rapped sharply against the windshield, startling Spiegel with the unexpected noise. There was the house, built in two stories in a faint echo of the Gothic style (not that any one of the three men driving up to it knew the word "Gothic") with tall narrow windows, all alike. It was L-shaped, and they could see for a moment both faces of the house. The sun was about to set behind them, and in the front of the house the windows caught the rosy light and reflected it back at them so that for the moment the name of the Bower of Roses seemed appropriate.

"Ready?" growled Klein.

"Yes," said Spiegel. Excitement had dried his throat so that he could only croak, but then he forced himself to assert himself. Klein's question made it appear possible that Klein was anxious to take the lead, with the obvious intention of claiming the credit later, and Spiegel was not going to have that.

"Follow me," he said, getting out of the car and marching up the steps with his hand on his pistol.

At the door they were met by Richter, Lucas's confidential secretary.

"I want to see the Brigadefuehrer," croaked Spiegel.

"Why?"

"Party business," said Spiegel.

"You could have spoken to the Brigadefuehrer on the telephone," said Richter, barring the way.

"I insist," said Spiegel, but his resolution was oozing out of him. Already he was trying to compose in his mind the speech he would make to excuse his coming like this with two killers of the Party to Lucas's house. Lucas might believe him.

There was a loud report at Spiegel's elbow which made him leap in surprise, and Richter fell to the ground. Kramer had shot him through the heart. At the back of the hall stood a large Chinese vase on a pedestal. It sprang into fragments at the same moment, the pieces clattering to the floor.

"Come on!" said Klein, pushing forward, and Spiegel realized that the bullet which had killed Richter had gone right through to smash the vase. They pushed on into the large sitting room beyond, crammed with furniture, where a white-faced woman stood to face them. It was Frau Lucas; Spiegel had often seen her before.

"What is it?" she asked.

"Where's your husband?" demanded Klein, walking towards her, pistol in hand.

"He is not here," faltered Frau Lucas. "He—he has gone to Berlin."

That was a lie, as Spiegel clearly saw. The presence of Richter in the house proved that Lucas was there, or had been until a moment before. He could think quite logically despite his trembling fear.

"Where is he?" he snarled, his lips wrinkling back from his teeth with the intensity of his feelings.

"He—he has gone," said Frau Lucas.

Klein swept the room with his glance, and hurried across to the door opening into the dining room. He had trodden in Richter's blood, and both his feet left bloody imprints on the carpet. There was no one in the dining room.

"Watch her, Spiegel," said Klein. "Come on, Kramer."

They rushed out of the room. Spiegel stood with his hand still on his pistol, but there was no need for such a precaution. Frau Lucas was a spiritless creature. She sank into a chair and put her face in her hands and wept, shaking with sobs. Within a few minutes Kramer and Klein were back again, herding two maids before them.

"He was here when we came," said Klein. "He hasn't left the house."

"Where is he?" demanded Kramer of Frau Lucas, but Frau Lucas, when she raised her tear-wetted face, working with fear, could say nothing at all. Klein swore vilely.

"Where is he?"

With his pistol he struck a sharp blow on Frau Lucas's wrist so that she cried out in pain, but still she said nothing.

"I'll do it," volunteered Kramer. "Watch the girls."

He stepped forward, pocketing his pistol, and slapped Frau Lucas on the face. Her head jerked back, but still she did not speak, and Kramer stepped closer to her.

"Bend back her nails," said Klein.

This was horrible. Spiegel could not bear it. For all his clarity of vision and keen forethought he had not imagined anything like this; just a clean killing. Frau Lucas screamed. Spiegel walked nervously out of the room. In the darkening hall Richter lay in his blood, and the fragments of the Chinese vase strewed the floor. Richter was dead; that could never be explained away, nor could what was happening to Frau Lucas. It was his life or Lucas's now. If Lucas were to survive, were to gain contact with Berlin, Spiegel and Klein and Kramer were all dead men. It might be a most unpleasant death, too. Spiegel felt his knees going weak at the thought.

Another scream from Frau Lucas, higher-pitched, agonizing. Spiegel wiped the sweat from his forehead with his left hand—his right still rested unconsciously on his pistol—and walked across the hall, through the open door opposite. This was both library and music room: shelves of books, a piano, a music stand. Oh, that frightful scream! Spiegel paced nervously on the thick carpet.

What was that? As he turned he saw that a section of the bookshelves was slowly swinging out. It was a narrow secret door, and within, his back to Spiegel as he peered out, was Lucas, a pistol in his hand. Automatically, Spiegel made the gesture. It was only yesterday that he had first practiced with a pistol, but now, despite his thumping heart and shaking limbs, one part of his mind worked fast enough though another part did not know what he was doing. His hand with the pistol in it leaped from his pocket. One shot into Lucas's back sent him reeling; with two more he sagged to the ground, and Spiegel went on firing into the prostrate body until the weapon was empty. It was all over in a matter of seconds, and instinct—the instinct never to reveal anything to a colleague without prospect of advantage—led Spiegel to close the secret door just before Klein and Kramer came bursting in. He was standing then, pistol in hand, over the body.

It was only a matter of days before Spiegel's prevision when he plotted the death of Lucas was proved correct.

The man who killed Lucas was held to have demonstrated Lucas's guilt; his bold initiative and his obvious
devotion to the Fuehrer was rewarded, in the reshuffling
that followed the Night of the Long Knives, by immediate promotion. He was head of the Seventh Bureau in
Lucas's place, and it was now only to be expected that
a man who worked as hard as he did, and who pos-
sessed that remarkable clarity of vision, should succeed
in making the Seventh Bureau even more powerful and
feared than when Lucas had presided over it. The
outwardly insignificant Kurfurstendam office under
Spiegel's management was like the tiny body of some
creature whose long tentacles, reaching out over vast
distances, insinuated themselves through any unguarded
crevices, and exuded a fatal poison if anyone were rash
enough to interfere with them. The bureau filched
power from Goering and the five-year plan, it filched
power from Canaris and his intelligence agencies, and
it even filched power from Himmler himself, as Spiegel
directed its activities not only into espionage, but into
counterespionage, and then into counter-counterespion-
age, working steadily towards the great moment when
the Fuehrer would listen to reports—injurious reports,
of course—regarding Himmler and his methods.

The Seventh Bureau was one of the agencies that held
the power of life and death, and a word from Spiegel
could send a man to the scaffold or into a concentration
camp; sometimes, naturally, that could not be done
without bargaining—Spiegel's enemy A could not be
murdered without sacrificing to Himmler Spiegel's ally
B. But still it was power, vast power, and Spiegel, wak-
ing in bed in the mornings, would sometimes wonder

whether it was not all a vivid dream, so exactly had he realized all his ambitions. He had enemies, of course, deadly enemies, for a man who held power under the Third Reich was the enemy of all who sought power or sought to conserve power; but he could deal with those, while reveling in everything that his starved childhood and his unemployed youth had lacked: the deference of the great, and the subservience of the little, power to promote and power to condemn, even medals and orders, and, beyond all this, the intense satisfaction, which never staled for a moment, of living (whenever he could spare time from the office) in the Bower of Roses. He slept in Lucas's bed and he ate at Lucas's table, and that was wildly gratifying, for he could always remember the fear with which he had regarded Lucas and the contempt with which Lucas had regarded him. And he had killed Lucas with his own hand; he could remember that and forget that it was pure chance which had presented Lucas's back to his pistol.

Ten years of gratification, of power, of what to a warped mind was happiness, was what Spiegel enjoyed; perhaps for those ten years he may be considered fortunate. He extended his power, he increased his happiness, while the Fuehrer extended the Reich. The Saar and the Rhineland, Austria and Czechoslovakia; Spiegel shared in those intoxicating successes. He knew the rather dubious delight that followed the conquest of Poland, and the equally dubious delight that followed the conquest of Norway, and he shared in the culminating triumph, the one that swept away all doubts, of the overthrow of France. The Fuehrer entered Paris as a conqueror, without any of the blood baths, like Verdun

and the Somme, that Germany had dreaded. The Fuehrer dominated the world; by his apparently magical
power he had raised Germany to a position which she
had failed previously to attain even at the expense of
millions of lives. And Spiegel shared in his dominion,
and he lived the life of a nobleman in the Bower
of Roses.

It lasted ten years, as has already been said, before
the unforeseen tripped Spiegel up. He did not anticipate the events of July 1944. It was not a question of
the defeats in Russia or of the landing of the Allies in
France; Spiegel made no pretense of being a military
expert. But he did not anticipate that there would be an
attempt on Hitler's life, and that that attempt would
fail. It had not entered into his calculations, and the
surprise of it unbalanced him so that he was taken by
surprise by the next development, which normally he
would have predicted with cold certainty.

The attempt on Hitler's life was revenged by a massacre compared with which the Night of the Long
Knives was only a trifle. Ten thousand people died
in four weeks; generals and priests, diplomats and
dancers, not only men, but women and children too,
whole families, sacrificed to the resentment of the
gloomy tyrant shut away in his headquarters in East
Prussia, who found some sort of satisfaction in looking
at films and photographs of the slow hanging of his
enemies.

Ten thousand people died; it is not surprising that in
that general massacre private grudges were paid off, nor
that ambitious men seized the opportunity to eliminate
those superiors who stood in the path of their promo-

tion. Spiegel could have predicted all that, easily, but he did not have time. The wave of arrests engulfed him at the very start, almost before he knew that the attempt had been made.

He was at the Bower of Roses on that July day. He was taking refuge from the sultry heat of Berlin; and the incessant air raids on the city had induced him to go there, too, for—as he told himself—they were distracting, and liable to confuse his otherwise clear thinking. He had sat with his wife Charlotte listening to the first confused accounts on the radio, and then he had spent a couple of hours on the telephone—not hours of unbroken talk, because in that period of excitement not even the head of the Seventh Bureau could command unrestricted use of all the long-distance wires he needed —and he was glad that he was absent from Berlin at this moment, where arrests and executions, betrayals under torture, were going on. His absence from the center of affairs would prove his lack of complicity, and if by any strange chance the conspiracy should still succeed he might still be able to disclaim any antipathy to the conspirators.

He sat at his dinner table, with Charlotte opposite him, feeling not too unsure of himself. His telephone calls had been well judged. He thought all would be well. It was comforting to sit where he did, with the red sunset bathing the landscape over which he looked from his seat at table. There was his own land, the green fields, the dark pine woods, and the glimmer of the lake through the gap. He tasted with pleased anticipation the soup that was put before him. Then he looked out of the window again and saw two trucks hurtling along the road, driving fast. He knew their type; he could make out the machine guns mounted above the drivers' cabs. The trucks vanished at the corner and then reappeared. They were heading for the house. There would be twenty SS men, fully armed, in each. He put down his spoon. He did not stay to say a single word to poor stupid feeble Charlotte, but he hurried out across the hall, and into the library where he opened the secret door and took refuge in the secret room within.

He stood just inside the secret door, resting his hands against it, listening. He heard the tramp of innumerable booted feet, in the hall, in the very library itself, upstairs, in the sitting room, everywhere. He heard loud voices— and one of them he could recognize—so that he leaned heavily, faint, against the door. It was the voice of Klein, one of his principal assistants (Spiegel had been too shrewd to have only one principal assistant) in the Seventh Bureau. Klein, the man who had driven the car on the Night of the Long Knives when Lucas had died; Klein, not a yard from where Spiegel was standing at the moment; Klein the ambitious, Klein the brutal— Spiegel knew now that he ought to have eliminated him a year ago at least, or earlier, as soon as the murder of Lucas had become such ancient history that Klein's account of it would no longer be damaging to his chief. If only he had had him arrested even yesterday!

There were other loud and brutal voices to be heard besides Klein's. Then through them all came the sound of another voice. It was Charlotte's, raised in a high-pitched scream. Spiegel heard the voice again, and then again, agonizing, frightful. Scream followed scream. It was no use torturing Charlotte. No one knew of the se-

cret room except Spiegel. He had even hunted out the
men who had constructed it, and he had seen to it that
they had met the fate of those who had buried Attila,
and without knowing why. Spiegel stood and listened to
the screams, almost inhuman now in their intensity.
They were frightful, unbearable. In his office Spiegel
had written words, had spoken sentences, which had
sent men and women to horrible deaths. But he had not
witnessed the results. Richter's corpse and Lucas's
corpse were the only two he had ever seen. In his office,
making his plans, Spiegel was always a man of steady
nerve and of cold resolution, but personally he was a
weakling, and he had always known it. He heard the
screams again, and found his hand had gone, without
his volition, to the catch of the door. Now, without his
volition, he was opening the door. Now he was coming
out into the library.

Less than a year later, Wolfgang Klein found himself
walking along a Brandenburg lane. He was tired, he
was hungry, he was ill, but he had to keep on walking.
The war was lost, the Fuehrer was dead, the Russians
were in Berlin—the Russians were all round him. Klein
had managed to get rid of his SS uniform; he knew too
well what happened to a man in that uniform if the
Russians caught him. No trial, just one single shot. So
now he was wearing an ordinary army uniform. He had
taken it from a corpse lying unexplained in a wood, and
the tunic had a bullet hole in it and bore an extensive
stain of blood, but it was far better than that SS uniform, for all that. It gave him at least a faint chance.
There could be no doubt that the Russians would seek

eagerly for the head of the Seventh Bureau, and would shoot him if they could lay their hands on him. In this uniform, with pay book and papers complete, he at least stood a chance of losing his identity and of being taken prisoner as a mere private soldier. Better even a Russian prison camp than a firing party.

His features were not too well known; it was hardly likely that any local informer would recognize him. Klein knew something about that ritual. In the villages and towns the Russians would find men ready to work for them. The Russian commanding officer would have each prisoner and suspicious character brought up before him in the presence of the local informer.

"He Fascist?" the Russian officer would ask in his childish German, and the informer would nod and the suspect would be led out to death.

Klein, even in his army uniform, did not want to run any such risk. He wanted to keep out of the hands of the Russians altogether. That was why he was creeping along the lanes like this, hungry, footsore, and tired— so tired that he could hardly think. He was a man of powerful build and great physical strength, but that strength was now exhausted. He could hardly drag his feet, at each successive step, through the sands of the lane. He staggered as he walked in the darkness, and his lips were caked with dried scum. He had not known that such weariness was possible.

All Germany—all the vast empire of the Third Reich —was in the hands of the Allies. There was no possible chance of his escaping out of it. The Americans were on the Elbe, he knew. He would stand a little more chance of life if he could make his way there and give himself up to them. But he would not risk it. The Elbe was fifty miles away and the Russians would be watching every possible point at which he could cross, and even if he succeeded there would be trials of war criminals, hangings and shootings.

What he ought to do was find somewhere where he could hide away, for months and months, until the Russian vigilance had died down and the American animosity had evaporated. Then he might at last emerge, find anonymity among the people—possibly even escape to the Argentine—and live. With all his faintness and exhaustion and hunger Klein still wanted to live. There was only one possible refuge open to him, and that was, absurd as it might seem, in his own house, where surely the Russians would be waiting for him. But what Klein knew and what the Russians could not know was that in the Bower of Roses there was a secret room, the perfectly planned hideaway. It was concealed between two partition walls between the library and the kitchen, and it was a place where he could live for months. Its window was one of a long row of Gothic windows in that wing of the house, and an active man could climb up to it from outside; no one was likely even to count from the outside the long line of windows of library and kitchen and ballroom and then, remembering that number, count the windows from inside and find they totaled one fewer. Inside there was just room for a man to lie down—God, how he wanted to lie down at this moment—among the other things that careful forethought had put there. There was a silent toilet, a water tap connected to the main supply of the house, and, above all, shelves and shelves of food, cans of every possible description, six months' food at least for a man, perhaps even a year's food. Klein felt hunger gnawing at him with renewed viciousness as he thought of that food. It might seem a mad plan to return to the Bower of Roses, of all places, and yet it was the best plan open to him. The Russians would certainly be there, but at night he could make his way in through the window with its cunning catch, and then he could rest, he could eat, he could drink. Klein stumbled forward with renewed strength as he thought of that. He did not even waste any strength in self-recrimination regarding his own lack of forethought in allowing himself to be in Berlin at the moment when the Russians came bursting over the Oder—a farsighted man, one with prevision, would have concealed himself in the secret room just before that event. As it was, his resolution and physical strength had enabled him to escape from the city during its nightmare end, out to this lane where he could plod along towards the Bower of Roses, stumbling with weariness, yet trying to keep his ears and eyes open for Russian sentries and patrols.

Klein reached the Bower of Roses the next night. It was before midnight that he sank down to rest for a while at the edge of the wood whence he could look out at the house, but he waited for three hours before he hoisted his exhausted body up onto his weary legs to attempt the last stage. It was not merely to rest himself that he waited. Between midnight and dawn would be the best time for Russian vigilance to relax, and besides he wanted to examine the situation for as long as possible beforehand. He watched lights come and go in the windows, the faint uncertain light of candles and lamps, for there was no electric power available, naturally. But there was one window that was never lighted; that was the one for which he yearned. The number of cars parked about the house showed that it had been taken as the headquarters of a large unit, a division at least, perhaps a corps, but that, too, was only to be expected. There was only the headquarters staff present, as far as he could see; no large fighting units. Then the flickering of an electric flashlight, off and then momentarily on, enabled him to see that there were sentries posted about the house; he was observing the midnight relief and was glad that now he knew where they were.

He waited for the next relief, and for an hour after that, before he bent his stiff and aching joints and moved cautiously forward out of the wood. It was not far; there was only a single wall to cross, and after that he proceeded on his hands and knees. He had to lie prone for several minutes, close to the house, while a sentry stood near him in the darkness, and then, when the sentry had moved off towards the corner of the house, he made his final rush, as quickly as silent movement would permit. He put one foot in the niche of the buttress, as he had long ago learned to be necessary, and heaved himself up, climbed another step, and then reached for the window catch. As he pressed it, silently, and swung open the window he congratulated himself on his luck. He got one arm and shoulder through the window, transferred his weight, and hung for a moment before a final effort pulled him through, his hands on the floor first, and then his knees. He fought off his exhaustion long enough to make himself stand, to wait by the window for a second or two to make sure he had not been observed, and then to shut it.

The necessity for that amount of self-control made the reaction even more violent when he allowed himself to relax. He lowered himself to the floor. He would not eat or drink, not daring to risk making a noise in this unaccustomed darkness, and in any case he was too weary to move. All he wanted to do was to rest, to rest. He lay on the floor with his head pillowed on his arm, a feeble stream of muddled thought coursing through his weary brain. He was here, safe for six months. There was a momentary pride as he told himself that this was the boldest feat of his career, taking refuge in the midst of a Russian headquarters, but that satisfaction was at once engulfed in the greater one that he no longer had to exert himself or keep himself alert. With his eyes closed again in the darkness he let himself drift off to sleep. In his sick weariness it seemed to him as if the whole floor of the room was gently and slowly swinging from side to side, not unpleasantly, lulling him to sleep.

His consciousness forsook him for a few seconds, and then he came back into the world abruptly as light poured in upon him and voices spoke. The door was open and a man was standing framed in the doorway; the pistol in his hand was plain to be seen even though it was in the man's shadow. It was pointing straight at Klein. And it was a Russian uniform that the man wore.

"*Komm,*" he said.

Klein blinked, stupefied; the only movements he could make were feeble and ineffective like the last flapping of a dying fish. A hand reached down and seized him by the breast of his coat and dragged him out into the library, his head bumping painfully on the edge of the door as he passed it. The hand tried to haul Klein to his feet, but was not strong enough. Another pair of hands came to its assistance and hauled him up, but he could not stand, and so they thrust him backwards into an armchair where he sat, still blinking in the light, and only slowly emerging from his befuddlement.

There were half a dozen Russians in the library, all with pistols in their hands. The senior one turned and gave an order, which resulted in the door into the hall opening and another man being led in, someone in a ragged black uniform. The half-grown beard, the mop of tangled hair, the dirty face, made recognition difficult, especially for a man as dazed as Klein. But the Russians stood aside, on either hand, so that the newcomer had a clear view of Klein, and Klein had a clear view of the newcomer. Klein's eyes submitted at last to being focused, and he saw who it was. Kramer, his chief assistant. They led him forward, closer, and the senior Russian officer pointed to Klein.

"He Klein?" he asked in his infantile German.

Kramer's eyes met Klein's for only a moment before turning away.

"Yes," he said. "He Klein."

"He Fascist," said the Russian with satisfaction, and he went on to speak in his own language to his colleagues.

Klein's brain was working a little more rapidly now. Kramer had known about the secret room from which Spiegel had emerged when they had come to arrest him, and there had not been time between then and the advance across the Oder to silence Kramer. And when arrested, Kramer had bought his life by offering to deliver into Russian hands the head of the Seventh Bureau, who figured high on the list of war criminals. Klein hated Kramer, but then he had always hated Kramer.

There were some private soldiers in the room, and at an order from the senior officer they came forward and took Klein by the arms and lifted him up from the chair. He stood there, sagging between them, and then they began to haul him out of the room, his feet dragging on the carpet. At the door they had to relax their grip on him to pass him through; and he was free to turn back and address the Russians for a moment.

"He Fascist," he said, pointing with one free hand at Kramer. "He Fascist."

Then they led him out of the house.

MIRIAM'S MIRACLE

Sturmbannfuehrer Schiller was a most conscientious and hard-working officer. He thought that on account of these qualities he fully merited promotion to a higher rank in the SS—his present rank was equivalent to that of major—but he did not allow the thought to make him discontented. Sooner or later his merits would attract the attention of the Reichsfuehrer, and promotion would be accorded to him as soon as that happened. Then he would become Obersturmbannfuehrer, Standartenfuehrer, even Brigadefuehrer—higher than that his modest ambition did not venture to soar. Until then he was content to do his work as thoroughly as he knew how, enjoying the satisfaction of the knowledge that he was engaged in work of momentous importance in the history of the Reich and of the race; it might well be termed a crusade, except that there had been an unfortunate religious motive urging on the original crusaders in their otherwise laudable enterprise, Nordics that they were, of exterminating the Semitics.

The present crusade of course had no religious nonsense about it, and that was all the more reason why it should be carried on conscientiously and efficiently. Not merely did this mean that Schiller should obey orders strictly and to the letter, but also it meant that he should devote thought to possible improvements, and that he should display a prompt and wise initiative, acting on his own inspiration if that did not conflict with the orders he received. That was the spirit of the Third Reich: loyalty, co-operation, and activity. Schiller was even careful not to admit to himself that his superior officer, Standartenfuehrer Merz, was a drunken, lazy and uneducated lout, quite unworthy of his present high position—that was one of those strange appointments which were so unaccountably noticeable here and there in the organization of the SS. Merz was supposed to exercise a general supervision over a whole group of concentration camps, of one of which Schiller was commandant, but actually his supervision was negligible. Merz was content to pass his days in swinish drunkenness, and to allow his camps to go on along the haphazard lines of their early institution, without thought of improvement. That did not suit Schiller, who sometimes had ideas. It was little use pressing these ideas on Merz, but luckily there were plenty of occasions when Schiller felt justified in acting on his own initiative, when he was sure that such action was not in contravention of standing orders. He wanted his own concentration camp to be a model of efficiency, and he was prepared to go to considerable lengths to achieve that ideal, for the sake of the Party, the race, the Reich, and the Fuehrer.

On one occasion he employed a day's leave to consult with his friend Fluss, who was manager of the Schultz Chemical Works just across the frontier in Silesia—they were going full blast, of course, on account of the war with Russia, and they made every kind of chemical one could think of. Fluss listened attentively to what Schiller had to say.

"I should have thought," was Fluss's comment at length, "that carbon monoxide, from what I know of it, would have done the job well enough."

"No," replied Schiller. "In theory it should be ideal, but in practice there are many difficulties, and with this new directive regarding building materials I do not want to have to build an entirely new hall. Besides, we were instructed a year ago to practice economy in gasoline, and it's surprising how many gallons of gasoline the motors consume for each operation."

"I see," said Fluss. "I'm no chemist myself, as you know, but I'll see what I can do."

And Fluss pressed his bell and barked an order at his secretary; the order brought into the office the head chemist of the establishment. He was a Czech, and until Czechoslovakia had been incorporated into the Reich he had been one of those intellectuals, wasting his time in idle speculation regarding the nature of the atom, and lecturing to students as idle as himself. The conquest had of course eradicated that plague-spot of dangerous talk and time-wasting discussion, but the Professor had been spared because he could be put to work usefully in the national task of rearmament—usefully as long as he was closely supervised, and stimulated by reminders as to what might happen to him if he were not useful.

The Herr Professor (they still called him that, in the Schultz Chemical Works, with amusing mock seriousness) was thin and aging. His worn face showed signs of the prolonged internal struggle he endured. He still felt burning shame at working for the enemies of his country, for the enemies of mankind. He felt burning shame at his weakness, about his fear regarding what might be done to him. One little taste of torture had been enough to make him docile. Since then he had worked well for his slave masters, proving surprisingly useful in the Schultz Works; but even in three years he had not reconciled himself to it. But he went on producing results for his masters, working hard with the utmost care—Fluss would interpret any slip as sabotage, and would hand him over to Schiller, and Schiller would order his friend Haupsturmfuehrer Braun and his Death's Head Unit to give him another taste of what he had already experienced, and the Professor could not bear the thought of that. So he listened carefully to what Schiller and Fluss asked of him, and he devoted his best thought to the problem.

"Something that can be cheaply produced," stressed Schiller, "a by-product if possible, which would otherwise be wasted."

He prided himself on his familiarity with so technical a term and his broad grasp of the problem.

"Yes, of course," said the Professor. "Let me see."

He was struggling with an attack of sudden sickness, but it would never do to allow these men to notice it. He thought about the Death's Head SS, and although that made him even more sick for the moment it enabled him to compel his mind to work.

"None of the by-products here would be effective," he announced at length, and then, seeing the expression on others' faces, he went on hurriedly, "but we actually produce the right substance here at the works. A good deal is used in various metallic reduction processes."

"So?" said Schiller.

"That is good," said Fluss.

He of course was not a working chemist, but an official of the Party. The position of general manager of the Schultz Works had been the reward for devoted party service during the lean days before the Revolution.

"It would not call for much?" asked Schiller, conscientious as usual.

"Oh, no," replied the Professor. "Only a trifling amount compared to the quantities we manufacture for commercial use. It would hardly be missed. I could calculate the correct amount if you would tell me the size of the—of the—"

"Of the hall?"

"Yes."

Schiller told him, and the Professor lifted his face to the ceiling as he worked out a sum in multiplication and division, while the other two watched him. They were both of them aware that to do a similar sum they would need paper and pencil, with no guarantee even then of reaching the correct answer. To watch a member of an inferior race doing the sum in his head was like watching a performing seal balance a ball on his nose; they could not do that, either, but they were of a race equally superior to the seal, and it made a good exhibition.

"A single kilogram would be sufficient," announced the Professor. "One kilogram of each of the two substances to be mixed together."

"Only two kilograms?" said Fluss.

"You had better be sure about it," said Schiller.

"I am sure about it," said the Professor. "Great care would have to be employed in the operation, of course. But with simple precautions the method would be safe enough."

"Safe enough?"

"I mean safe enough for the operators. The instructions could be quite brief."

"Then go and make up a package for the Herr Sturm-bannfuehrer," said Fluss, "and write out the instructions for its use."

When the Professor had gone—he could vomit when he was outside—Schiller thanked Fluss for his help.

"It is my duty to do all I can to aid the Party," replied Fluss, simply. "I suppose you will want a weekly supply?"

"I can make out a formal application and receipt for your files," offered Schiller.

"Not worth the trouble," said Fluss with an airy wave of the hand. "Books and files and receipts—what are they in these days of national effort?"

Schiller did not press the matter; he knew that a certain elasticity regarding files and receipts had been part of the reward for Fluss's services, as was the case with many of the party jobs, and it was not for him to question the infinite wisdom of the Fuehrer in permitting such an arrangement.

Meanwhile, Miriam was praying for a miracle. She had been praying for a miracle for days now, ever since the *Einsatzkommando*—the Extermination Squad—had seized her and a dozen others from her village and forced them on board the train: cattle trucks, already crammed with people. They were hungry and thirsty and some of the old people died each day of the journey, but each day more and more people were forced into the cattle trucks. They were jammed together; at the halts the dead were taken out and hastily buried, while the living drank from the puddles beside the tracks—terrified, desperate people who wept bitterly at the thought of their coming fate, while Miriam prayed for a miracle.

Not merely for a miracle that would save her life, but a miracle that would bring an end to the horrors that had descended on the world like an eternal night. No effort of man seemed capable of ending these horrors, and Miriam prayed for the intervention of God. She was young, and she ventured to pray not merely to the God of her fathers, who had brought down the walls of Jericho in ruins, but to the God who had filled Saint Elizabeth's apron with roses, and to the kindly Mother whose intercession had in other, less hateful centuries modified some of the dreadful things mankind had set out to do. She prayed, amid all the unspeakable horrors of that train journey, humbly; she knew that intellectually she was not very bright, and that with her harelip she was displeasing to men, but her faith told her that her prayers might be listened to even so.

But the miracle did not occur during the journey. The train reached its destination at a siding in a forest, and guards with whips and rifles forced everyone out and along a road cut amid the trees. Barbed wire hedged in the road on either side, and then they came to a clearing in the forest, where a double nine-foot fence of barbed wire surrounded a large collection of buildings. It was not very far from the railway siding to the gate in the fence; even the old and the sick were able to walk that distance, thanks to the whips of the guards. There were more guards at the gate, and at the angles of the fence there were towers where guards were stationed with machine guns; guards in black uniforms with the Death's Head insignia that even Miriam knew about.

Inside the gate, in an open square, the shouts and blows of the guards halted the helpless mob. They stood still, a thousand of them, young and old, men, women, and children, clinging to each other; those on the outside could look down the radiating roads between the buildings, but they could see few people, for the inmates were all out at work in quarries and mines and factories. Then further orders were shouted. Some of the guards could speak the languages of the prisoners, a few words at least, and with blows from the whips and much pushing and dragging they formed up the prisoners into orderly lines with spaces between them. There were women among the guards, wearing the same uniform and insignia, and their whips hurt just as much. They helped to keep the lines under control; for in the process of forming the lines families and friends were divided, and children tried to run across from one line to another, to rejoin their mothers, and there were blows and screams as this was prevented. The prisoners stood in their lines as a young officer walked along with fountain pen and writing pad. He looked into each prisoner's face in turn and made a notation on the pad; it took a long time and some of the prisoners fainted as they stood. But when the others saw what happened to the first to faint they held their fainting neighbors up on their feet.

Where Miriam stood in line she found herself with people whose acquaintance she had not made on the journey; on one side of her was a middle-aged couple and on the other, a young mother with two small children. The middle-aged woman was sobbing hysterically, but the young mother was engaged in keeping her children quiet for fear of the whips. They had all glanced at Miriam but had not spoken to her; she was used to that—strangers did not readily enter into conversation with a girl with a harelip. She still prayed for a miracle, wildly, feverishly.

When the prisoners had been counted a new order was shouted along the lines.

"Clothes off! Clothes off!"

It was repeated in all languages, but at first the prisoners could not believe that it was really meant. They were soon convinced of it, however. The guards had pistols at their belts as well as whips in their hands; one woman was singled out by a guard and the order was bawled at her several times, and when in her bewilderment she did not obey, the guard drew his pistol and shot her, twice. She fell down and only writhed a little. The prisoners who did not see the deed heard the shots, and heard the wail that passed down the lines—"He has shot her! He has shot her!"; and after that, in face of the menace of the drawn pistols of the guards, and with the order ceaselessly shouted at them, the prisoners obeyed. Men and women; mothers hastened to strip their children; with the threat of instant death before their eyes the prisoners overcame their shame and modesty. Naked they stood in their lines, with their pitiful heaps of rags at their feet. Miriam stood among them, among the women sick with shame, and like them she tried to cover herself with her hands. But perhaps she did not suffer as much as the others. She had spent her young lifetime ashamed to have people look at her face; and perhaps she was already coming to believe in the imminence of the miracle for which she prayed.

A small group of uniformed officers appeared on the square, and the young officer who had done the counting saluted them with the upraised hand of Nazism. He was proud to be able to report to Sturmbannfuehrer Schiller that there were nine hundred and seventy-four living prisoners. The manhunt had been most successful. Schiller received the report, and then, with the doddering old doctor beside him, and a group of guards following behind, he began to walk along the lines. The doctor looked over each prisoner in turn—a fleeting glance—and some he pointed out to the guards following with a nod of the head and jerk of the thumb. It was not a very high proportion that he selected in this way. A child might have guessed that he was picking out the able-bodied, the labor for the mines and factories, but the children there did not guess it. It was only the very best that he picked, the able-bodied men—not many of those—and the sturdy women, for the death rate among the slave labor was high even so, and it was not worth while bothering with inferior material.

The children beside Miriam screamed when their mother was taken from them, and tried to follow her, but the guards beat them back, and the aged people on the other side of them held them and tried to comfort them. Miriam could not do so, for the jerk of the doctor's thumb had singled her out as well, but when she started out of the line Schiller caught sight of her face (the doctor only looked at bodies) and thrust her back again. That sort of stuff was not worth preserving even for slave labor, and Miriam knew perfectly well the motives that actuated him.

Those whom the doctor indicated picked up their bundles of clothes, under the orders of the guards, and went off down the lines, the reluctant or the stupid helped on their way with well-aimed kicks, and at the far end of the square they formed another group, the lucky ones, who had been granted a longer life, some days or weeks or perhaps even months of toil and starvation. The ones left in the lines understood. Their fate, they knew, was to be the deathhouse, the awful institution that had been discussed in the villages and towns with shuddering fear ever since the Nazis had come bursting over their borders. There were many of them who stood shrieking with hysterical terror, directing their screams to the unresponsive sky to which they lifted their faces, but the others stood paralyzed and numb, amid the wailing of the children; cries which might be expected to be heard across the oceans.

The selection was finished and the lucky ones were already marched off to their barracks, when at Schiller's order the guards began to herd the others together and drive them slowly, after picking up their clothes, towards the long low buildings at the edge of the square. They went slowly enough, reluctantly, under the lash of the whips and the menace of the pistols. The pistols meant death this moment, and the journey to the shed meant a few minutes more of life, and so they went, with dragging steps, and screams of terror, their nakedness forgotten.

A painter of the Middle Ages, depicting lost souls being herded into Hell after the Last Judgment, would not have made use of those hideous drab surroundings, nor would he have included children among the damned, nor would he have clothed the devils in black nor armed them with whips and pistols. Nor would he have thought to include among the damned a young woman with a harelip.

Miriam went along with the others. Somehow, incredibly, she still had hope. She was still praying for a miracle. It still did not seem impossible to her that there should be one. Like the others, she looked up at the threatening autumn sky. If there was no sign of hope there as yet there still might be one. Then this awful procession would end, and then these pitiful victims would tread triumphant over the prostrate bodies of their tormentors.

But the miracle was long in coming. The head of the procession reached the door of the building. Here there was dreadful fear, and the leaders hung back pitifully, as the guards round the door made them deposit their clothes in a pile and then go in over the threshold. Blows and threats were necessary here. In the slaughterhouses of Chicago they have a Judas goat to lead the sheep to the butcher; he goes free each time and apparently enjoys his work, but Schiller had not been ingenious enough to think of some similar device. The first among his victims had to be kicked and shoved with violence in through the door; and the others were driven in after them, pushing the leaders towards the far end of the building although they did not want to go there, but wanted to stay near the entrance. Slowly the crowd was driven in, old men and old women and children, the cripples and the diseased, more and more and more of them, packed tight. Miriam was in the center, with naked flesh pressed close against her naked flesh, but she was no more conscious of it than were the others. This would be the time; this would be the moment. Then the door was slammed shut, and the windowless building lost its faint light and became pitch dark inside; the instant coming of darkness was marked by a climax in the screaming within the building, and Schiller outside gave an order to the member of the Extermination Squad who stood by the machine.

That was when Miriam had her miracle. The screaming around her stopped, and the roof was torn wide open to reveal blue skies and streaming sunshine—sunshine so bright that momentarily it hurt her eyes. But only momentarily; she was in bliss. The people around her were laughing with the joy of it. The world had changed, and the horror and bestiality had vanished. When she put her hand to her face she was not surprised —although the absence of surprise did not diminish her joy—to find that her harelip was healed and she was as beautiful as the day.

Outside Schiller heard the screaming stop. The Czech Professor had been right. Schiller ordered the door to be opened and glanced in.

"Give it plenty of time to ventilate," he warned the guards. Some of them were already handling the pincers and shears with which they harvested the rings and the gold teeth from the dead before they were taken to the crematorium next door.

"You won't find much this time," said Schiller. "They were a poor lot."

THE PHYSIOLOGY OF FEAR

Dr. Georg Schmidt was not a young man, and perhaps because of that he sometimes found it hard to believe that this was a real, permanent world in which he was moving and living. He had qualified as a doctor in the days of the Kaiser, before 1914. A man who had vivid recollections of the Hohenzollern empire, with all its tradition and appearance of permanence, and who had then seen the Weimar Republic come and go, and who had lived through the inflation and through several revolutions, abortive and otherwise, found it a little difficult to believe in the prospective existence of the Third Reich for a thousand years, which its supporters predicted for it. This was especially the case because Schmidt was of a cynical turn of mind, with his cynicism accentuated by a scientific education. But his cynicism was not of the right type to be of use to him under Hitler and the Nazis, considering the sort of work he was called upon by them to do. For he was appointed a surgeon in the SS, and posted as medical officer to the Rosenberg concentration camp. There he could inspect the water supply and sanitary arrangements, combat epidemics, and do all the things he had learned to do thoroughly between 1914 and 1918. However, a medical officer in a concentration camp had other duties as well, which were hard to perform; there is no need to enlarge upon them, except to comment that perhaps the easiest duty was to advise upon the issue of rations so that the prisoners had the minimum diet on which life could be sustained.

All the hideous things that Schmidt had to do, he had to do. That was simple. The Party cast a cold eye upon any man who flinched from obeying orders; those orders came down from the Fuehrer himself, and they were not rendered any less sacred by the fact that they were transmitted, interpreted, and expanded by a number of officials before they reached Schmidt. Those officials held their authority from the Fuehrer, and a man who caviled at doing what he was told by them to do was guilty of treason against the Fuehrer, against the Reich, and no fate could be too bad for him—even though anyone who knew the sort of fate that was meted out (and Schmidt saw it meted out) might have thought it was too bad for anyone. Schmidt knew all about the gallows and the block, the torture cells and the gas chambers, so he did what he was told, moving in a world that was like a bad dream, hoping that what he saw and did was not really happening; hoping that sometime soon he would wake up and find it was only a dream after all.

So, when his leave came round in the summer of 1940, he welcomed it with as much gladness as he had done in the old days of 1917. He handed over to the doctor who came to relieve him; he packed his fiber suitcase, saw that his papers were in order, and started off for the railway station and for the city that he called "home." He had few relations—his wife was dead—but his brilliant nephew Heinrich had invited him to spend his leave at his house there, and Schmidt was looking forward to that. Young Heinz was a product of the new generation, he knew—because of the exigencies of the service he had seen little of him lately—but Schmidt was quite certain that he was a nephew to be proud of. He had not only qualified in medicine, but he had attained a Doctorate of Science, and even now, with Germany mobilized, he was still a civilian, holding a research fellowship at the university—a sure proof of the esteem in which he was held. Schmidt had read the early papers he had contributed to the university "Transactions" and had glowed with pride. His nephew was clearly destined to be one of the great physiologists of the world, a man whose name would always be remembered. Schmidt would have liked to have been a famous research worker himself, and he found a vicarious, almost a parental, pleasure in his nephew's achievements.

Heinz himself opened the door to him when he rang the doorbell after a tedious night journey across wartime Germany.

"Welcome, Uncle," he said, relieving him of his suitcase.

Heinz was everything an uncle might wish for, tall and blond and handsome, smartly dressed, vigorous— he had all those advantages as well as being a man of brilliant mind. And his wife, Caecilie, was a desirable niece, too—a very pretty girl in a uniform not too obtrusive. She made Schmidt welcome with the utmost kindness and hospitality.

"You look tired, Uncle," said Caecilie. "We must try and remedy that while you are with us."

Schmidt glowed with something like happiness as they showed him his room and saw to his comfort. More than ever at that moment did his duties at the Rosenberg concentration camp appear like a bad dream.

"You and I have an appointment for luncheon, Uncle," said Heinz.

"Indeed?"

"With Standartenfuehrer Kroide. The president himself."

There was a humorous twinkle in Heinz's eye as he spoke. He could see the incongruity of having a Nazi official as president of a university which dated back to the Middle Ages.

"How is it that I am invited?" asked Schmidt.

"I mentioned to him that I was expecting you," explained Heinz, "and that you were my uncle."

"And he wanted to meet the uncle of the great physiologist?" said Schmidt. "I have attained fame at last."

"Turn round, Uncle," said Caecilie, clothes brush in hand. "I want to brush your shoulders."

On the way to the university, walking through the streets multicolored with uniforms, Schmidt asked his nephew about his work.

"Is it still intercellular osmosis?" he asked.

"No," said Heinz. "It's a larger project altogether. Immensely larger, and it may prove to be of great importance to the Reich."

"Is it a war secret?"

"The results may be, when we see what they are. But

there is no need for secrecy at present. I'm working on the physiology of fear."

"Very interesting."

"Very interesting indeed. The government is of course assisting the university. I understand that the Fuehrer himself knows about my research. At any rate, it is the government, of course, that is providing me with suitable subjects."

"That must be a great help," said Schmidt.

"Oh yes, of course. It would be hard to conduct such research without a plentiful supply. And the university has been most co-operative. I have a thousand cubic meters of laboratory space for my use. Actually I am using the laboratories once used by Liebig and Hertz—remodeled, of course."

"That's a compliment in itself," said Schmidt.

The university had a long and honorable record for scientific research. The world was at least a healthier place, if not a happier, as a result of the labors of the university's scientists.

"I'll take you round and show you after lunch," said Heinz.

"Thank you. That will be very interesting."

Schmidt was not quite sure that he wanted to be shown. The physiology of fear could hardly be investigated without causing fear, and he did not specially want to be shown terrified animals; many animals, obviously, with the government undertaking to supply them.

"I suppose rats and guinea pigs are unsuitable for your investigation?" asked Schmidt.

"Of course," said Heinz, and then the glow of enthusiasm in his face died away as he changed the subject and pointed across the road. "Here's the president's house."

Standartenfuehrer Kroide was no scientist, not even a scientist in uniform. As head of the university he represented the Ministry of Enlightenment and Propaganda, naturally. It was his business to see that German youth not only was educated along the lines most useful to the Reich, but also that it was not educated along the lines that were improper.

"We are proud of our young man, here," said Kroide, indicating Heinz. "A splendid example of the new growth of scientists of the Third Reich. One of our earliest, but with the example he has set he will not be our last."

Kroide was a man with the same personal charm as the head of his ministry. He could talk charmingly and interestingly, and at luncheon he entertained Schmidt, who sat at his right, with a vivid account of the success of the new system of education, a success demonstrated by the correct thinking of all the new generation, and resulting from consistent methods employed from earliest childhood.

"Your nephew himself was distinguished as a boy in the Hitler Youth," said Kroide.

"I remember," answered Schmidt, and that was only true as he said it. He had forgotten about Heinz's early activities, and he thought Heinz probably had forgotten them too. The notion crept into his mind that it might be difficult to retain the ideas of Nazism when one was a true scientist, but he put it hastily aside. Some people would have thought it blasphemous; Schmidt knew it was dangerous.

When lunch was over Kroide shook Schmidt's hand.

"I have no doubt your nephew is impatient to carry you off," he said. "He wants to get back to his experiments as well as to show you his work. I hope when your leave comes round again you will let me know so that I can again have the pleasure of entertaining you."

"Thank you, Standartenfuehrer," said Schmidt.

Walking from the president's house over to the laboratories, Heinz began to go into further detail regarding his work.

"Thanks to the Reich and the Fuehrer," he said, "I am able to investigate the subject in a way that has not been possible before. There could never be exact measurements of any sort, and I expect that is why fear has never been analyzed physiologically until now. All that is known is contained in two paragraphs in any standard textbook of physiology, as I expect you remember, Uncle."

"A line or two about the suprarenals," agreed Schmidt. "A little about blood pressure."

"Exactly. All vague and unscientific. But now we can tackle the subject quantitatively and scientifically. Some of the results I have already obtained are most significant and illuminating."

Schmidt wondered vaguely how fear could be measured with any exactness, even if intelligent animals, even if monkeys were employed. But now conversation was interrupted, as they were passing through doors guarded by SS sentries, and crossing courtyards similarly patrolled. There were salutes in plenty for the Herr Professor, and it occurred to Schmidt that the government must be anxious to keep the research a secret to provide these guards.

"And here we are," said Heinz, holding open a door for Schmidt to pass through.

There were guards here as well, in the long well-lit laboratory, guards in black uniforms with Death's Head insignia; guards carrying whips—it was they whom Schmidt saw first, and the sight puzzled him. There were seated workers and standing workers; the seated workers, each at a separate bench, were covered with scientific instruments of all sorts applied to their naked bodies. Schmidt could guess at the use of most of them; there were instruments for measuring blood pressure, and instruments for measuring the amount of air inspired, for recording respiration and heartbeat. Beside each seated worker another, standing, was diligently employed in noting the recordings. The nakedness of the seated workers was surprising. Most surprising still was the sight of the apparatus before each one, when Schmidt came to notice it. Each one had a roulette wheel in front of him, and was spinning it, and was dropping the little ivory ball into the basin as he spun it. Schmidt could understand nothing of what he saw, and looked at his nephew in complete bewilderment.

"What is happening here?" he asked. "Where are the animals?"

"Animals?" said Heinz, "I thought I made it plain to you that I do not use animals. These are my subjects. These."

He indicated with a sweep of his hand the twelve naked men sitting at the roulette wheels.

"Oh," said Schmidt, weakly.

"With animals," said Heinz, and something faintly professorial crept into his manner as he spoke, "it would be quite impossible, as I told you, to obtain quantitative results of any value. For those, intelligence on the part of the subject is necessary. Besides, I have already proved that there is almost no analogy between the physiological effects of fear in animals and in man."

"But what are they doing?" asked Schmidt.

"It is simple," explained Heinz. "As practical ideas usually are. They spin their roulette wheels, as you see. The numbers that turn up are immaterial. It is the red and the black that count.

"Yes?"

"It is explained to each subject when he is brought here that when he spins eight consecutive reds it is the end for him."

"The end?"

"These subjects are all people who are destined for liquidation, of course. They might as well be usefully employed first. And some of my most valuable data are acquired at the autopsies, as you can understand."

"Yes."

"And so these subjects are spinning their roulette wheels, and that is how I get my quantitative results. It is remarkable how exact they can be. A man spins a single red, and he hardly cares. Two, and he is not much more concerned either. With the third and the fourth the physiological effects become more marked, and when it reaches seven the graphs show a very steep incline."

"I suppose so," said Schmidt.

He told himself that he was in a real world, with these

things actually happening in it, and yet he found himself still wishing wildly that he would awake from the nightmare. There was a sharp crack and a cry of pain from the far end of the room, and Schmidt looked in that direction in time to see a guard turn away from one of the subjects after dealing a blow with his whip.

"As the number of consecutive reds increases the subject grows reluctant to go on spinning the wheel," explained Heinz. "Compulsion has to be employed with most of them."

"Naturally," said Schmidt. He knew perfectly well that if he blazed out in protest he would be proved not to be wholeheartedly for the regime—he might even find himself sitting spinning a roulette wheel.

"And yet the psychology is as interesting as the physiology," went on Heinz. "There are some who spin feverishly as if anxious to reach the end. We have even had a few who anticipated it, killing themselves in their cells at night—a nuisance, because it means a premature termination of the results in their case."

"That must be a nuisance," said Schmidt.

"The psychological findings are of course being analyzed by another department," said Heinz. "Old Engel has a team of assistants at work on them. But psychology is by no means as exact a science as physiology—it can hardly be called a science at all, can it?"

"I suppose not."

"With half these subjects," explained Heinz, "it is made clear to them that when they spin their eight reds they will meet their end by the quick SS neck shot, all over in a second. The other half are told that it will be a more painful process, prolonged as far as the SS can manage it. But it is quite surprising how little difference that prospect makes to the physiological results—the subjects really do not look beyond the fact that they will die when they spin their eight consecutive reds. In fact I am thinking of discontinuing that part of the investigation, for the treatment administered by the SS brings about a serious confusion in the eventual findings at the autopsy. My work is more important than that of the psychologists."

"Of course," said Schmidt. He wanted to sit down, but Heinz went on talking, enthusiastic about his subject.

"Most of this apparatus I designed myself," he said. "This one here provides a continuous record of the rate of sweat secretion. The curves I am obtaining with it sometimes offer interesting contrasts with the graphs of blood pressure and respiration."

He bent over to show the apparatus to Schmidt, standing close to the subject, a heavily built and swarthy man, who at that moment uttered a groan of despair.

"Seven, I see," said Heinz. "You notice how the blood pressure rises?"

The subject struggled on his stool—it was only then that Schmidt noticed that the subjects were leg-ironed and chained in their places. A guard came sidling up, his whip whistling shrilly as he swung it in the air, and at the sound of it the subject subsided.

"Spin," said the assistant who was taking the recordings, and the subject spun the wheel and dropped in the ivory ball, which bounced clicking against the metal studs.

"Ah, black," said Heinz. "Most of his curves will show an abrupt decline at this point."

Schmidt felt relief that it had been black this time.

"Some of these subjects last literally for weeks," commented Heinz. "It takes that long sometimes for them to spin their eight consecutive reds. And yet there is very little flattening of the curves—you would be surprised at the consistency of the results. I'll show you some of my graphs in a moment."

"That would be very interesting," said Schmidt.

"One at least of my preconceived notions has been disposed of already," said Heinz. "I had formed a theory regarding possible fatigue of the suprarenals, but I've proved myself wrong. It was one more example of the necessity to correlate relevant facts before forming a hypothesis."

Heinz twinkled at the memory; he did not mind admitting the human weakness.

"Yes, it is very necessary," agreed Schmidt.

It was in the adjoining smaller laboratory that the graphs were kept. Heinz dilated on them with enthusiasm as he displayed them to his uncle, the saw-backed curves, continuous lines and broken lines, dotted lines and starred lines, lines of different colors, a dozen curves on each sheet for the various physiological measurements of an individual subject, mounting irregularly upwards towards an abrupt end; each sheet told the physiological history of the last days of a man.

"Extremely interesting," said Schmidt, trying not to think about that part of it.

Back at the house Caecilie was quite indignant with her husband.

"Uncle looks more tired than ever, Heinz," she said. "You've worn him out today. I'm sorry, Uncle. These scientists never know when to stop when they get started on their hobby. Why don't you have a little rest before the evening meal?"

Schmidt certainly needed a rest, and at dinner fortunately the conversation was not directed towards the physiology of fear. The Luftwaffe was at that time engaged upon the subjugation of England, so there were plenty of other subjects to discuss—the results of the day's air fighting, the possibility that England might accept the Fuehrer's magnanimous offer of peace without the necessity of submitting to invasion, the future of a world enlightened by the ideas of Nazidom. It was only at intervals during the rest of Schmidt's stay that Heinz discussed his research work. Once was when Caecilie had displayed some feminine weakness or other.

"Odd," said Heinz, when he was alone with his uncle, "how inconsistent women can be. Some of the curves I've obtained with women subjects at the laboratory show the most remarkable variations from normal. The psychologists have seized upon them to help prove some of their theories. And I have to admit there's something to be said for them, too."

And another time, after they had listened to a broadcast speech by Baldur von Schirach, Heinz talked about race in connection with his research.

"Of course," he said, "most of my subjects are Poles and Czechs. I expect you noticed that they were all of the Alpine or Mediterranean types. Even the non-Slavs were of those types. Naturally there are Semitics as well in plenty, but to make my research more complete I need Nordic types."

"Naturally," said Schmidt.

"And Nordic types are not so readily available. But I have asked the president to make the strongest representations on the point, and he is doing so. A Nordic type may commit a murder, perhaps. Or there is always the chance of a few Norwegians."

"Of course that's possible."

"And then I shall get a new set of curves. And the post-mortem appearances should be most interesting."

"Yes."

It was a great surprise to Schmidt to hear his nephew talking the Nazi nonsense about race, about Nordics and Alpines. It was hard to believe that a scientist, a scientist with a good mind—even though completely heartless in his work—could possibly give any weight at all to those old theories. Schmidt had to remind himself that Heinz had been exposed to that sort of talk since his boyhood, had hardly known a world where Nordic superiority was not assumed as an article of faith—at least publicly—by everyone. That upbringing of Heinz's would largely account for his utter heartlessness, too. So that to Schmidt it was hard to decide which was the greater strain, to stay and listen to his nephew talking about his physiological research, or to go back to his nightmare duties at the concentration camp. But he had no choice; when his leave was up he had to go back to Rosenberg camp, into the dreadful conditions there, and he had to do the dreadful things he was called upon to do.

It was in the winter that he received a letter from Caecilie. He recognized the writing on the envelope, but the postmark was strange.

They have taken Heinz away [wrote Caecilie]. Two SS men came and arrested him at night and of course they did not say why. Uncle, I am very worried and I am writing to you to ask you to help because you are in the SS. I am going to post this letter in another town in case they see me posting it and open it. Uncle, please help me. Please find out where he is and try to help him. He was always a good Nazi, as you know. He has never said anything or thought anything that the SS could say was treason. I pray you to help me, Uncle. He would have been an army doctor gladly except that the ministry decided he would be more useful in research. *Please help me.*

The first thing that Schmidt did after reading that letter was to burn it. It was dangerous enough to be related to a man who had been arrested by the SS; to be asked by the man's wife to help was even more dangerous. And there was nothing he could do, either. The SS kept its secrets, and no insignificant surgeon could hope to be admitted to them, and if that surgeon began to ask questions it might be—it would certainly be—too bad for him. Schmidt did not even answer Caecilie's letter; her mail would undoubtedly be opened and read, and he could not risk even expressing sympathy for a man whose guilt was obvious because of his arrest. He worried about it, though.

The following summer, after the invasion of Russia

had begun, Schmidt attended a selection parade in his
official capacity.

"A hundred and twenty," said the camp commandant
to him; from the little office they could hear the shouts
of the guards and the Kapos—the internees who did
duty in return for a little more food and a little less ill-
treatment—as they formed up their party for the parade.
"There will be five hundred present, so you can take
one in four. A few more than a hundred and twenty will
not matter."

This was the worst of Schmidt's duties, to select the
men and women who were to die in the Rosenberg gas
chamber. Those were the times when he almost thought
he would rather have the gas chamber for himself—almost. That "almost" might explain how he had come to
be selected as surgeon in the SS, and posted to a concentration camp; the SS picked their instruments carefully, and they had noted how fear had forced Schmidt
into accepting duties progressively more revolting.

Schmidt drank a glass of schnapps, saw to it that his
uniform was correct, and stepped out into the blinding
sunshine on the parade ground. Perhaps it was not as
bad to select men victims as women. Usually the men
made less commotion about it; many of them tried to
appear brave, and were ashamed to show emotion before
their fellows—some of them, not very many, would try
desperately to make a joke when they were selected.
And, on the other hand, they were often so worn down
with harsh treatment that they were apathetic. Schmidt
hoped that would be the case now.

He walked along the line. Behind him the guards followed to herd away the victims he selected. He had to

choose one in four. He might merely have indicated every fourth man, by pure chance, but he dared not do so, lest the anomalies should be too glaring. If he picked those who were still fit and able and left the old, the sick, and the worn-out it would be noticed. He had to exercise some care in the selection.

He did not look at the faces; he could not. He looked at the bodies. The diseased, the old, the starved; he had to keep his head clear and his mind active so as to keep count and maintain the proportion of roughly one in four. He pointed to those he selected and passed on. Behind him there were groans of despair; sometimes hysterical screams; the sharp sound of blows; sometimes even a shot as some desperate man resisted and was given his end on the spot. Halfway down the line Schmidt heard a sudden whisper from the line; a single word:

"Uncle!"

He looked up from the body to the face. It was Heinz; but if the word had not been spoken he would not have recognized him. The growth of dirty beard alone was a disguise. And Heinz had lost some of his teeth and his nose was not quite straight now, and his cheeks were hollow, with the cheekbones standing out. Schmidt looked down again at the scars and sores on the body. If he had not looked at the face he might well have selected Heinz for the gas chamber, young and vigorous though he had recently been.

Neither man dared show further sign of recognition. Luckily the SS men were some yards behind and had not heard the whispered word. Luckily the men on either side of Heinz were old and could be picked as victims—luckily Schmidt's mind was clear enough for him to think of that, lest they should talk and should involve him in Heinz's catastrophe. Schmidt passed on and left Heinz standing in the line, unchosen. Schmidt was shaking with the shock, after his moment of clear thinking, and it was all he could do to complete the parade.

As medical officer Schmidt had access to the files in the central office, and after a decent interval he went to examine them. He went through the card index elaborately, looking at many names, so that the corporal on duty there would not guess what was the real object of his search. Heinz's card was there, but—as Schmidt fully expected—it told him nothing of importance. There were only dates and the names of camps. Heinz had been in two bad ones before coming to Rosenberg, which accounted for the scars and the sores. But there was no indication of what his offense had been—that was only given on the cards of prisoners who were guilty of crimes in the old sense. The SS kept its secrets. Schmidt came away from his examination of the files knowing no more than he had known before. Nor was he going to make any further inquiries. No one ever inquired about an SS prisoner; nobody wanted to be thought interested in an SS prisoner's fate.

Schmidt was about to have leave soon again, and it called for an effort to decide what he should do then. He had heard from Caecilie that she had been conscripted into factory work, but her house was still open to him, of course. There was almost nowhere else that he could go, and he went, eventually, and Caecilie made him welcome as always. The house was by no means entirely hers now, as a number of technical workers had been billeted in it—to Schmidt that was something of a relief, because it restricted conversation about Heinz. Caecilie could only speak about him when they were quite alone, and then no louder than a whisper. Schmidt was sympathetic but noncommittal; he had decided after prolonged thought not to tell her about his encounter with Heinz. It would do her no good, and it might do her a great deal of harm. She would want to know all about him, how his health was and how he looked, and Schmidt neither wanted to tell her nor could he trust himself to lie convincingly. Moreover, Caecilie would expect him to do something to alleviate Heinz's fate, and Schmidt knew that to be impossible. He could not bear having to tell her that.

And there was the question of his oaths; at the time of his induction into the SS he had sworn to keep the secrets of the organization, and he had sworn a further oath never to reveal to the outside world anything about what went on in concentration camps. Secrecy made the SS more dreaded than ever, and it was even possible the SS did not feel happy at the thought that the outside world should know about the nature of the punishments it inflicted. Schmidt had no scruples about the oaths he had taken, but he did not want to violate them by telling Caecilie what he knew. Caecilie might at any time be arrested, and under questioning by the SS she would certainly reveal—Schmidt knew about that questioning—anything Schmidt had told her. It was best not to tell her anything.

But because of the prickings of his conscience in the matter he decided in the end to do what he had had in the back of his mind for some time. There was a risk about it, but it was the best he could manage. He sent a polite note to Standartenfuehrer Kroide at the university, telling him of his presence in the city on leave, and —he had not really expected it, but only hoped for it— received in return an invitation to luncheon.

It was the usual large party, and Kroide was his usual charming self, the perfect host. It occurred to Schmidt, as he listened to the conversation, that these parties were one tiny strand in a vast spider's web spread all over the country, in the center of which was the spider, Dr. Goebbels himself, attentive to all the vibrations that passed along the strands. There was wine, there was the freest of conversation, and after such a party Kroide would be able to pass along a good deal of information regarding the attitude of the local intellectuals.

Today there was no lack of a subject to talk about. The army was pressing far and fast into Russia, and the communiqués were blaring victory. There could be no doubt that the Russian colossus would soon be beaten to the ground. No army could long endure the defeats the Fuehrer was inflicting on the Russians. They would collapse, and that would be the end of Germany's last rival save for England, impotent across the sea and fast being strangled by the U-boat campaign. There were some quite amusing jokes about what the Fuehrer would do with Stalin when he fell into his hands. Standartenfuehrer Kroide sat beaming as he listened to the talk, and he let it be understood, by his significant reticences, that he could, if security did not forbid, add much to the conversation, and that, as a high official of the Ministry of Propaganda, he was cognizant of many secrets regarding the further surprises the Fuehrer had up his sleeve for the enemies of the Reich. He beamed and he drank wine, mellowed by alcohol and victory. It was after lunch was over, as the guests still stood chatting, that he addressed himself to Schmidt.

"Too bad about that young nephew of yours," he said.

"My nephew Heinrich?" asked Schmidt, without committing himself.

"Yes. I once had great hopes for him. I thought he was a talented scientist and a fervent friend of the Reich, but to my disappointment I found he was neither."

"I am sorry about that, Standartenfuehrer," said Schmidt. It was safe to be sorry about Kroide's hurt feelings, even if it was not safe to be sorry about Heinz's fate.

"The silly young fool," said Kroide. "Not only was he completely wrongheaded, but he wanted to proclaim the fact publicly."

"How very extraordinary!" said Schmidt.

"Yes, indeed. He told me he had completed that piece of physiological research on which he was engaged— you remember—and I was quite delighted. I encouraged him all the time he was writing his paper regarding his results, and I looked forward to the time when it should be completed."

"And did he complete it, Standartenfuehrer?"

"Yes. Naturally I did not read it; it was far too technical for me. I forwarded it, just as it was, graphs, statistics and all, to Dr. Goebbels's office, as was my duty, of course."

"Yes?" Schmidt hoped he was not displaying too much interest. Despite the wine which made his head swim he tried to put exactly the right intonation into what he said.

"I was really only concerned with security—I thought it was possible, or even likely, the paper might contain material that our enemies also could find useful. It was a routine step, to decide whether it would be desirable to publish the paper in the university 'Transactions.'"

Kroide took off his spectacles and polished them, and blinked shortsightedly at Schmidt.

"It was a great shock to me," went on Kroide, "when the teletype message came in ordering me to suppress everything to do with your nephew's paper. The SS, of course, had already arrested him by the time the message reached me."

"How shocking!" said Schmidt. He still did not dare to ask the obvious question, but he waited hopefully, and his hope was not disappointed.

"Yes," said Kroide, almost with regret. "The SS had no choice but to arrest him and put him where his ridiculous theories could do no harm. Do you know what the madman had written?"

"I simply cannot guess," said Schmidt.

Kroide leaned forward confidently and tapped Schmidt on the chest with his spectacles.

"He had it all wrong. I even think he might have had insane delusions. He thought he had proved that fear had exactly the same physiological results with Nordics as with the lesser races! Can you imagine anything more insane or more treasonable?"

"No," said Schmidt.

INDECISION

There were medal ribbons across the Baron's chest, and there was a cross hanging from his buttonhole, and he wore the epaulets of a major general, but what was more important was that he wore the crimson stripes of the General Staff. Even to someone who did not know the Baron personally that would be the most important thing about him; anyone with good fortune and bulldog courage might rise to be a major general, but it called for much rarer qualities to be appointed to the General Staff. To pass the rigorous tests necessary, a candidate had to be blessed both with brains and a capacity for hard work, and furthermore a suitable combination of these two, for a high proportion of either one would not compensate for a deficiency of the other. A certain quality of character was necessary too; not merely an unremitting diligence, but a selfless kind of diligence that prompted the candidate, regardless of his own future, to devote all his efforts to making the German General Staff the finest in the world and the army that it directed necessarily the finest in the world as well. The watchful people in high positions in the General Staff were always on the lookout for men with these qualities, and whoever was discovered to possess them was promptly rewarded, not necessarily with promotion, although that might be incidental, but with work and more work, responsibility and more responsibility. One other factor was desirable yet unnecessary, and that was noble descent. Plenty of people from bourgeois families had risen to high rank on the General Staff, but it helped to be of blue blood, and the Baron's blood was the bluest of the blue. That was why he was called *the* Baron, when there were thousands of barons in the army of the Reich; he had been called that ever since he was a subaltern, and although it was a nickname conferred by the accident of birth one could be prouder of it than of some of the other nicknames which had begun to be whispered in the ranks, like the "Hitler Youth General," or the "Yes General," or the "Lackey General."

It was many years ago that the Baron had passed into the General Staff. He was aging now, and it was certain that he would retire (if he lived long enough) with no higher rank than his present one. He would never carry the baton of a field marshal; he would never even be a full general because he had been found wanting in other qualities. For a brief interval he had been entrusted with the command of a division in the field, and it had soon become apparent that he did not possess the bloody resolution, the dash, and the infectious personality necessary to a man commanding fighting forces; the staff needed him, and the field army emphatically did not. He had been brought back and re-established in his office, where he could do work that few others could do, and thereby influence the operations of the army, for good or evil, far more than any general com-

manding a division—more than any general commanding an army corps, or even an army, for that matter.

Because the Baron was a man with a remarkable
brain; it would have been remarkable in any man, and
it was quite astonishing to find such mental powers in
someone of blue blood. To anyone unacquainted with
the conventions that ruled the German Army, it would
be still more astonishing that the man with such a brain
should go about with a shaven bullet-head that gave
him a brutish look, and with a single eyeglass screwed
into his right eye to flavor the brutishness with an appearance of vapidity.

There could be no doubting his powers, though. As
a subaltern, the Baron had enlivened dreary evenings in
the mess by impressive little demonstrations—he could
run swiftly through a pack of fifty-one cards and an-
nounce without hesitation which was the missing one.
Long and complex tables of establishments were as
familiar to him as the buttons of his uniform; admiring
—and exasperated—subordinates used to say that he
knew every nut and bolt necessary for the equipment of
an armored division, and the weight of every tool allo-
cated to a bridging company. With this remarkable
memory was combined a logical and mathematical mind
that could calculate the ultimate resultant from a host
of converging factors.

It was in consequence of these abilities that the Baron
had been in charge, for a long time, of the military management of the railways—the most complex and sensitive
section of all the work of the General Staff. From Bor-
deaux to Warsaw, from Copenhagen to Rome, not a
train moved without an order for which the ultimate

responsibility lay with the Baron. It was a task that gave
full play to his co-ordinating abilities. He had to bear
in mind not only the permanent factors, like the shortage of coal and of rolling stock, and the necessity of
keeping the mine traffic ceaselessly on the move, but also
the constantly fluctuating factors, such as the damage
done by Allied air raids and the repairs that had been
effected. The bottleneck of Ulsen, the complexities of
Ham; he had been familiar with those for years, and at
the same time he had always at his fingertips the details
of the military demands of the Eastern front; for it was
he who directed the torrent of men and materials thither
—the torrent that like a river losing itself in the desert
poured in that direction to evaporate amid the fiery heat
of war. At one and the same time he might be faced
with the demand for routing a couple of army corps to
Bessarabia and the necessity of evacuating the civilian
population of Hamburg, and it was the Baron's business
to see that the two operations were economically per-
formed even if fog or snow or flood came unexpectedly.

Today—a flaming summer day, although he was
hardly aware of the fact—he had some delicate problems to solve. He sat at his desk in his office thinking
them out. The walls were covered with maps, but he did
not have to refer to them; they were there so that he
could illustrate his orders to his subordinates, or explain
to other generals not as logistically minded as he the
incompatibility of their several demands. A very large
troop transference had to be planned, for Fuehrer Headquarters was now coming round to the idea that the
Anglo-American landing in Normandy was a serious invasion and not a mere feint designed to bring about the

evacuation of some other sector of the European coast.
If Fuehrer Headquarters did not change its mind—as it
often did—the correct action to be taken would be to
gather up all available divisions and fling them upon the
invading army, to scrape together every man, every gun,
and every tank that could be spared from other duties,
to move them across the continent with the utmost
rapidity, and to strike with the utmost force before the
Allies could build up their strength.

There were German divisions in France not yet engaged; von Rundstedt and Rommel and Fuehrer Headquarters were deep in a triangular argument about the
advisability of moving them, and where. The Baron had
to calculate the chances of whose opinion would prevail
—and then he had to superimpose the chances of the
Allied air actions allowing those troops to move by rail
at all. Yet allowance had to be made for rolling stock in
case of sudden demand. Other things were more easily
calculable; there were divisions earmarked as a mobile
reserve in Norway and Denmark and Friesland, and even
here in the environs of Berlin; pitifully few after the
disasters in the East, and yet enough to make it a tricky
business to thread them all through the network of
worn-out railways already carrying as much traffic as
exhausted equipment and personnel could handle. The
problems involved were of exactly the type to suit the
Bron's mind, and he was devoting himself to them with
something of pleasure, and with the disinterestedness of
a surgeon performing a delicate operation. The patient's
wife might be sitting in the waiting room weeping, waiting for the result, but the surgeon would give her no
thought. The Reich might be torn to pieces, but that

was not the Baron's business at the moment; he had to concentrate on moving certain divisions in a certain direction.

Moreover, there was a small but unusual complication. Mussolini, *il Duce,* was on his way to pay a state visit to the Fuehrer. In extreme secrecy his special train was starting today, winding its slow way over the Brenner, carrying *il Duce* all the way across Europe from his puppet principality in Italy to Fuehrer Headquarters in East Prussia. Not only the secrecy but the precautions against assassination complicated the move. Routing train and pilot engine to an exact rendezvous with the Fuehrer, across the lines of communication of the struggling Central Army Group, called for careful consideration.

So the Baron was not too pleased when his office door opened and the Count came in. The Count was a lieutenant general, and a lofty figure at the Staff Headquarters round the corner in the Bendlerstrasse, and he was a lifetime personal friend as well; the pleasure of seeing him nearly counterblanced the Baron's irritation at being interrupted in his work. But it was possible, that the Count had suggestions to make, or news to transmit, or orders to pass on, with an actual bearing on the problems at hand. The opening question seemed to indicate this.

"You have seen the new Fuehrer order?" asked the Count.

"Directive 112? Yes, I've seen it."

"You're working on it now, I suppose," said the Count.

"Yes," said the Baron.

The Count turned to study one of the maps on the wall, so that when he spoke again his face was averted, which might account for a stilted hollowness of tone in what he said next.

"I see the 98th Armored comes under your orders."

"Yes," said the Baron.

The 98th Armored was a division that had been nearly destroyed in Russia during the spring, and had been brought home to Parchim to be reconstituted, re-equipped and remanned. It was almost ready for service now—Fuehrer Headquarters declared it quite ready and had detailed it for transfer to France.

"Are you routing it through Berlin?" asked the Count, his face still averted.

"I haven't decided yet. But I don't expect so."

Wittenberge would probably be the better route, although there was something to be said in favor of Berlin with the Hamburg network so badly crippled and all those ammunition trains heading east.

"I see old Keil is in command," said the Count; he turned back from the map to face the Baron again.

"I didn't know that," said the Baron. "How is he?"

"Well enough," answered the Count.

Keil was an old friend, too, dating back to the days of the Kriegsakademie.

"His wife's hair is red this year," supplemented the Count, with a grin.

One half of the Count's face was less mobile than the other; the plastic surgeons had done amazingly good work after he had received that frightful shrapnel wound—there was no perceptible scarring, and they had given his face symmetry, but even their best efforts could not result in a completely natural appearance. There was something rather ghastly about his grin, which could hardly be due to the fact that they were talking about Wilhelmina Keil—Frau Generalleutnant Keil—whose amiable eccentricities were well known.

"What about Barbarossa?" asked the Count. "They are under orders too?"

"Yes," said the Baron.

"Fully equipped, I suppose? The cream of the new recruits? New Tiger tanks?"

"Of course," answered the Baron.

Barbarossa was an SS armored division, reconstituting itself in the same way as the 98th; the SS nowadays managed to secure the best of everything available. With its headquarters at Nauen Barbarossa it was within an easy day's march of Berlin.

"You'll be sending them first, then, I hope," said the Count. "Route them via Stendal. Give the old 98th a chance."

"The Tommies hit the railway bridge at Rathenow in the last raid. You ought to remember that," said the Baron. "It'll be three more days before it'll carry any traffic."

In ordinary circumstances it would be the natural route for the Barbarossa division traveling west from Nauen. As it was it would be more economical as well as quicker to send the 98th ahead through the bottleneck.

"I'd forgotten that," said the Count. It was remarkable how much concern he displayed over such a small detail as the relative times of arrival in action of the two divisions. "The road bridge is still intact, though.

Send Barbarossa by road as far as the river. It can en-
train on the far side easily enough—all the ramps in
the world in the sidings there."

"That would be sensible," said the Baron, "But—You
know as well as I do about the fuel situation."

Coal and rolling stock might be in desperately short
supply, but motor fuel and oil were scarcer still. No conscientious staff officer would move an armored division
by road when it was easily possible to move it by rail.

"Yes," said the Count meditatively. That wound of
his certainly gave the oddest expression to his face. Then
came a burst of candor. "You see, Baron, the first armor
to arrive will undoubtedly go into Dietrich's corps. You
know how old Keil stands with relation to Dietrich.
Sepp will have him relieved in two days—out of uniform, even, perhaps."

SS General Sepp Dietrich was a hard man, and the
Baron was vaguely aware of friction at some earlier
period between Dietrich and Keil. It might be possible
that Dietrich would take the opportunity of paying off
an old score if he found Keil under his command. And
Keil was, after all, one of the old army, while Dietrich
was Dietrich.

"I see," said the Baron.

"Send Barbarossa through first—Sepp will be glad to
have only SS troops in his corps. Then Geyr von
Schweppenburg will have Keil and the 98th. Geyr and
Keil are good friends."

"I would like to," said the Baron. "It's a pity about
the bridge."

Even to do a good turn for Keil he could not issue

orders that would mean wasting a whole day's fuel for an armored division.

"Tommy's air force!" said the Count. "Even Rommel couldn't escape them."

"Rommel?" asked the Baron.

"Good God! Haven't you heard? They got Rommel in his car two hours ago—he's badly wounded; doubtful if he'll live. Didn't you know? Von Kluge is taking over personal command of Army Group B."

"Rommel wounded!" said the Baron. The situation in the west might well be considered hopeless in that case. Rommel might have fought a good delaying action at least, but not fussy old von Kluge.

"You're so wrapped up in your damned trains," said the Count. "You have no thought for anything else. I don't believe you're human—I never have thought so. Even when we were young—"

"Rommel wounded!" repeated the Baron; his sick astonishment was proof that he was perfectly human. And yet, as regards his personal duty, it did not matter who was in command of Army Group B; what he had to do was to move the reinforcements earmarked by Fuehrer Headquarters into the sphere of command of the Commander in Chief west. Whether it was Rommel or von Kluge who handled them in action was none of his concern.

At this moment there was a distraction; Colonel Fink came into the room with a file.

"The Hamburg returns, sir," he said, and then, after a glance at the Count, "You've heard the news, sir?"

"About Rommel? Yes, I've heard it."

The Baron was already fidgeting with the file. He

had been waiting for it before completing his plans; Rommel wounded or Rommel in good health, those divisions had to be moved. And even though the news was disturbing, that logistical brain of his was at work, adjusting timetables one against another, and fretting because in the absence of the Hamburg data definite conclusions could not be reached. The Count had turned back to look at the map again.

"It's bad, sir," said Fink, and it was quite an effort for the Baron to realize that Fink was still talking about Rommel's wound, so rapidly had his mind reverted to its own problems.

"Undoubtedly," said the Baron. "I'll be ready to give those orders in an hour, Colonel."

"Very well, sir."

Fink withdrew, and the Count turned to face the Baron again.

"You'll route Barbarossa via Stendal?" he asked.

"I don't see how I can," replied the Baron, a little puzzled.

"Not even after the news?"

"I don't see how that affects it."

The Count looked round the room with a hint of desperation; half his face revealed his emotion while the other half remained wooden. Then he looked round the room again; this time it was clear that he was not seeking inspiration but was making sure he would not be overheard. He came close to the desk and lowered his voice. "Isn't this the time when we should try to save what is left?" he said in a low voice.

"If that were possible," said the Baron, puzzled that the Count should make such a point regarding whether

Keil should come under Sepp Dietrich's command or not, but also guarded because the Count was clearly being guarded as well.

The Count stepped back from the desk again; his monocle slipped from his eye—ever since his wound he had found difficulty in keeping it in place—and dangled by its ribbon. He replaced it carefully; seeing him do so was infectious, like seeing someone else yawn, and the Baron put his own hand to his own eyeglass, which was a mere rimless lens, devoid of ribbon or chain, fixed apparently permanently under his almost hairless eyebrow—people used to wonder if he slept with it in place. It occurred to the Baron that they might be two members of a secret society making the society's secret sign to each other, and then he realized that there was a tiny piece of truth in the idea, for the single eyeglass screwed into one eye was the almost exclusive prerogative of members of the nobility attached to the General Staff—life would be hard for any bourgeois, at least until he reached the rank of full general, who ventured to wear a monocle. His brother officers would rend him with ridicule.

Fink came in again at this moment.

"Fuehrer Headquarters are coming on the wire, sir," he said. "The field marshal will be through to you in three minutes."

"Very well," said the Baron.

"Then I'll leave," said the Count.

The Baron rose and stood at attention, as was the due of an officer one grade higher than his own, even though he was a lifetime friend. Fink brought his heels together, and then, stiff as a ramrod, marched the two steps to the door to open it. The Count hesitated before he passed through.

"Remember what I said," was his last remark, and then he was gone.

The door had hardly closed before the telephone bell jangled, three times, abruptly, indicating that it was the left-hand desk telephone to be answered, the one on the direct wire to Rastenburg. The Baron picked up the receiver and announced himself. At the same time he nodded to Fink, who hastened to the auxiliary desk at the far end of the room and picked up the extension there, spreading his notebook to record the conversation for the Most Secret pages of the telephone log of the Railway Headquarters.

Keitel's hard metallic voice was clearly recognizable.

"The Fuehrer has decided to leave the 202nd where it is," said Keitel. "But he will make the 409th available. All the other orders stand unchanged. Prepare the necessary routings—have you done so already?"

"Not yet, sir."

"Then do so at once. Those divisions must be on the move tomorrow morning."

"Yes, sir."

"I shall want a full report," went on Keitel. "Stauffenberg is flying here on the twentieth, the day after tomorrow. He can bring it with him. A full movement sheet and timetable. I want time to look through it before the Fuehrer Conference."

"Yes, sir."

"Staff officer, repeat those numbers."

"Two—zero—two," said Fink into his telephone, with

the greatest care in his diction to eliminate all chance
of mistake. "Four—zero—nine."

"Correct. Good-by."

Fink and the Baron replaced their telephones.

"I'll confirm the move-warnings, sir," said Fink.

"Very well."

Now the decision had to be made; that should be
simple enough, for the Baron's mind had had some
hours now in which to put all the data in place. Five
minutes should suffice for him to decide everything—
the substitution of the 409th from Rendsburg for the
202nd from Tondern actually simplified the problem.
He might as well begin to dictate the directives at once.
A few rapid sentences, and a hundred thousand men
and nearly as many tons of equipment would begin to
roll towards the west, cutting smoothly and cleanly
without turbulence across the vast stream of drafts and
munitions flowing daily to the east. But there was the
Count's suggestion to be borne in mind. Or to be dismissed without further thought. No officer with a strict
regard for his duty would contemplate using up a day's
fuel just to preserve Keil from the attentions of Sepp
Dietrich. The Baron had done little jobs often enough
for those of his kind, but only when all the other circumstances had been in strict balance. When there was
no concrete reason to prefer A to B, the Baron had naturally decided in favor of A when there was a "von" in
front of A's name. Yet here there was a very concrete
reason, and no friendship for Keil—not even that past
but happy friendship with Wilhelmina Keil—could
weigh against it. The strange thing was that the Count
could ever have thought it could, that he should have

expended the time and trouble of making a personal appeal. He had really been urgent about it, quite pressing.

It could be done, of course. If the Baron were to send Barbarossa by road across the river the keen minds at Fuehrer Headquarters—Keitel and Jodl—might dwell upon that clause in the orders for a moment, might spend one second questioning its advisability, but they would decide in the end—would decide at once—that the Baron could not be wrong; they would decide that his accurate judgment and weighing of all the pros and cons—whose significance they could not determine for themselves—must be relied upon. He could do it. He could move Keil through Berlin and Barbarossa through Stendal. Then—then—the Baron stirred uncomfortably in his chair. Then there would be a moment when there were no SS armored troops, almost no SS troops at all, in the vicinity of Berlin, while Keil would be close at hand with the 98th Armored. An interesting point. Very interesting indeed. That would be on the twentieth of this month, the day after tomorrow. The twentieth? The day after tomorrow? That was the day when Stauffenberg was to make his report at Fuehrer Headquarters. Stauffenberg! The Baron moved again in his chair. It was something more than the heat that made the palms of his hands wet, so that he wiped them nervously on his handkerchief. Stauffenberg was of blue blood, like the Count. There were dozens of Stauffenbergs, all cousins —his own great-uncle had married into the family. But this was Claus Schenk von Stauffenberg, the fiery active member of the family, whose restless vigor had not even been curbed by the mutilations he had undergone after

the explosion of a land mine in Africa. Stupid old Stieff
had mentioned once Stauffenberg's restlessness and dis-
content as well as his ability. And then there was the
link with that other group, those odd people who, de-
scendants of the fighting heroes of previous wars, debated ethics or dogma or theories of government, barely
existing under the strained toleration of the Fuehrer—
Moltke and Yorek von Wartenburg and those others of
famous names. There were ties of blood, of common dis-
content, between them and Stauffenberg, and through
Stauffenberg to the Count—and through the Count to
Keil. He had heard that Moltke had been arrested a
short time ago. The tension must be mounting to the
breaking point. So was it just coincidence that on the
day Stauffenberg was due to report personally to the
Fuehrer the Count was trying to replace the SS troops
in Berlin with an army division—and an army division
under Keil's command? Coincidence? The Baron's
hands were wet again. There were other discontented
people in Berlin at this moment. There were Beck and
Witzleben, who had held the highest positions in the
army and had been retired. They still made appearances
at the Herrenklub and at the ministry. Could it all be
coincidence? What was it the Count had said when he
was leaving this room a quarter of an hour ago? Something about "trying to save what was left." Did that
refer merely to trying to save the army from further
domination by the SS? The Count's expression, the
Count's manner; had they been quite normal? Yes? No?

The Baron, sitting solitary in his office, found himself
confronted with reality, more surely than if Death himself had stalked into the room to stand before the desk

with his bones gleaming in the sunshine. Reality; the Baron was an office soldier, as his brief experience in the field had proved. Those divisions that he moved about on his maps were not assemblages of men, living men of flesh and blood, of lusts and aspirations, of loves and hates and personal happiness and misery. They were only "divisions," colored pins on a map. When a division became "battle-worn" that did not mean that ten thousand men had suffered agony and death; it meant that a pin of another color had to be stuck into the map instead. The Baron had drifted entirely out of touch with reality; perhaps that had been an advantage during his tenure of the railway command. His remarkable mental powers had done nothing to keep him in the world of reality; actually they had acted the other way even when Stalingrad was lost; even when El Alamein was fought. But now he was face to face with reality again, reality so intense that he had to wipe the sweat from his hands and then from the hairless folds of the back of his neck. Death, agonizing and humiliating, might be awaiting him; the Baron had no illusions about the fate which an infuriated and frightened Fuehrer would deal out to anyone involved in a conspiracy against his rule. He had to decide what to do, and he had to decide quickly —Fink was waiting in the outer room for his orders. If he brought Keil's division down to Berlin he would be making a contribution to the success of the conspiracy— if there *were* a conspiracy. But the conspiracy still might not succeed. In that case there would be the strictest investigation, and his motives for ordering that particular move would never withstand Himmler's pitiless analysis.

It would be safer to issue normal orders. Safer—yes,

certainly, for should the conspiracy succeed, should the regime be overthrown, he could always say that it had never occurred to him that the Count had any special motive in making that request regarding Keil. Yet if he brought Keil down to Berlin the presence of the 98th Armored might make the difference between failure and success for the conspiracy. The SS police would not dare move in that case, or if they did the 98th would exterminate them. The SS would be exterminated whether they moved or not; the streets of Berlin would run with blood —the Baron faced reality again.

If there were a conspiracy blood would run in rivers, in rivers if the conspiracy succeeded and in rivers if it failed. And some of it might be his own blood. Lives were at stake, perhaps including his own. Not lives represented by numbers written on a casualty return, either. The lives of the Satanic Fuehrer in the Rastenburg headquarters, of Keitel of the metallic voice, of Jodl and Himmler and Goebbels; those lives on the one hand, and on the other the lives of the Count, of Stauffenberg, of Beck and Witzleben, his friends. And his own life too; it was strange how difficult it was to make that fine brain of his really think about that matter. The Baron forced himself to imagine himself being led before a firing squad; he forced himself to think of a sudden pistol bullet into his stomach which would leave him writhing on the ground in agony. He simply could not bear to think of such things.

The thought of something happening that would bring the present regime to an end stirred even the mentally insulated Baron to the depths; it aroused every emotion. Not only did it set his mind working fast, but it worked upon his bulky and lethargic body. He felt a quickening of his heartbeat and his respiration; he crossed and uncrossed his legs repeatedly, fidgeting in his chair. The thought was hideously attractive, like some female vampire of old legend. To end the agony through which Germany was passing; to save the army —the most vital institution of all Germany—not only from the Russians and British and Americans but from the Fuehrer and his minions; that was something to be longed for with all the passion of which the Baron was capable. But the danger was terrifying. Even to think of that demoniac personality at Fuehrer Headquarters made a man shudder. Inhuman, merciless—and cunning; facile in every shift and subterfuge, suspicious, savage; who would dare even to cross his path, let alone rouse him to the paroxysm of insane rage that would be the inevitable result of a move counter to his ideals, threatening his authority, imperiling his life? Torture and death would be the fate of everyone involved, and for everyone related by blood to them. That was something no one could face. The Baron's mind shrank away from such thoughts, just as it shrank away from the unhappy memory of his divisional command in Poland.

Save for that dreadful episode his life during Germany's agony had strangely been a satisfactory one; as military administrator of railways he had been doing a difficult job well, better than anyone else could have done it. His active logical mind had always been fully employed, and the moments of weariness had been made happy by the knowledge that he had made no mistakes, had wasted nothing, had kept his head clear in the face of myriad complications. Now he was like a chess master looking up from a study of the board to see that the spectators were drawing daggers.

The door opened to admit Fink.

"The orders, sir?" asked Fink.

"Oh God!" said the Baron. There were drops of sweat on his face which he mopped off.

Fink glanced just sufficiently obviously at his wrist watch to remind his chief of the passage of time.

"Very well then," said the Baron, desperately. "I'll dictate them now."

On the afternoon of July 20 the Baron was at his desk as usual. It was an even hotter, more stifling day. His eyes were on the clock on the wall; he was looking at it as though mesmerized. The two hands were together, indistinguishable. It was an instant's calculation for his mind to work out that in that case it must be sixteen point four minutes past three o'clock. But the hands seemed to be not merely indistinguishable; they seemed to be inseparable. The minute hand did not seem to move, so slowly the seconds were passing. The Fuehrer conference was usually over by two o'clock. By two-thirty on most days, or by three at the latest, he received his telephone call from headquarters. Keitel or Jodl or one of the junior staff officers at O.K.W. would transmit him his orders, telling him of the Fuehrer's decisions as far as they concerned him.

The wide strategic gestures the Fuehrer had made on the map were translated to the Baron in the form of directives, and he had to translate those into logistic terms—one careless sweep of the Fuehrer's pencil might mean reversing the direction of travel of two hundred trains. It was hardly ever later than three o'clock that

the first call would come through, and now it was sixteen point four minutes past three—no, he could call it
seventeen minutes past three now. Had Stauffenberg
succeeded in whatever it was he had planned—if he
had planned anything at all? The Baron's hand went
out to the telephone, and then he drew it back again.
He could not trust himself; he did not know what to say
over the telephone that would not commit him one way
or the other. To telephone might imply a guilty fore-
knowledge, but not to telephone might imply exactly
the same. How hot it was! His clothes were sticking to
him. Now it was half past three; he would wait until
quarter to four, and then he would telephone.

Here was Fink, agitated and excited; his hurried entrance started the Baron's heart pounding wildly. Fink
hardly gave himself time to click his heels.

"If you please, sir—"

"Y—yes?"

"The Home Army has been alerted for immediate
duty."

Then something had certainly happened.

"By whose orders?" The Baron hoped his voice did
not quaver.

"Orders of the Commander in Chief, Home Army."

"You are sure of this?"

"I put a query through to the Bendlerstrasse, sir,"
said Fink. "The reply was 'all orders of the Commander
in Chief, Home Army are to be obeyed.'"

"Who did you speak to?"

"Colonel von Stauffenberg, sir."

Stauffenberg! Back from Fuehrer Headquarters?

"You're sure it was he?"

"Oh yes, sir. I knew his voice."

"If those are the orders from the Bendlerstrasse then they must be obeyed," said the Baron at length.

"The Bendlerstrasse" was the universal term for the General Staff Headquarters, an eighth of a mile away from the Railway Headquarters. It was the source of all military authority in the absence of orders from the Fuehrer and O.K.W.

A knock at the door made both men jump. It was a junior officer, one of Fink's assistants, not privileged to enter without knocking. "Fuehrer Headquarters coming through on the wire, sir!" he said.

The Baron grabbed for the telephone; the receiver beat against his ear with the shaking of his hand. Fink took up the extension telephone.

"Who is that?" said the earpiece instantly, in the hard unmistakable voice of Keitel. The Baron announced himself.

"This is Keitel. You know my voice?"

"Yes, sir."

"You are to obey no orders from the Bendlerstrasse. None. You understand? None. And no orders from the Commander in Chief, Home Army either. Understand?"

"Yes—yes, sir. If you please, what has happened?"

"Nothing serious. You are to disregard all orders that do not emanate from me personally."

"Yes, sir."

The telephone went dead instantly, leaving the Baron and Fink staring at each other, the instruments still in their hands.

"I don't understand, sir," said Fink. "Shall I get through to the Bendlerstrasse?"

"No. Yes. No."

It was an incredibly serious matter to be told to disregard orders; an army that did so would fall into chaos, would melt into a formless mass like a wax figure in a furnace. Keitel was the direct representative of the Fuehrer; but the Bendlerstrasse was the direct representative of the army.

That knock at the door again; the junior officer reappeared.

"The Bendlerstrasse on the telephone, sir."

"Who is it speaking?"

"Count von Stauffenberg, sir."

"Very well."

There could be no harm in answering the telephone; that did not necessitate obeying any orders that might come through on it from the Chief of Staff of the Home Army. The Baron and Fink picked up the instruments from their desks, and the Baron announced himself.

"Good afternoon, Baron," said the telephone. It was Stauffenberg's voice, of normal pitch and modulation—perhaps there was a touch of lightheartedness in it, as there often was. "No orders from Fuehrer Headquarters is authentic. You are not to obey any such orders."

"I—I do not understand."

"Field Marshal von Witzleben is now in command. The Reich is in danger and the army has its duty to do."

Witzleben! All possible doubt as to the existence of a crisis disappeared with that name. If there were such a thing as an opposition to the Fuehrer, von Witzleben would be at least the titular head of it. The mention of the name introduced another complication; Witzleben as Field Marshal was senior to Keitel. If any military precept applied in the present situation, a soldier would obey von Witzleben rather than Keitel.

"Did you hear what I said, Baron?" asked Stauffenberg's voice, as airily as ever.

"I heard," said the Baron.

"Quite likely you will receive contradictory orders from Keitel," went on Stauffenberg's voice. "Field Marshal Keitel has no authority. Is that quite clear, Baron?"

"Not—not quite."

"It is a clear, definite order. You are to pay no attention to anything Keitel says. Lakaitel's day is over. So cheer up. Good-by."

The telephone went dead. If it were really true that the day of Lakaitel—the Lackey General—were over the army would rejoice. But clearly there was a clash in progress between the two forces, a clash that could only end in the death of every single supporter of the losing side. And it was impossible to guess from the data at present available which side would be the losing side. The Baron went back through his memory over his actions up to the present, and felt a momentary relief at deciding they had been entirely correct. But the Fuehrer was merciless—a creature without pity, with no more thought for his victims than a tiger. But Stauffenberg of the airy voice; he would be merciless too. That light manner concealed a will of steel and an unrelenting determination. The Baron thought of firing squads and torture chambers.

Then he recovered himself with the realization that Fink was still staring at him. The play of emotion over his face must have been quite obvious.

"Very well, Colonel," he said, making every effort to

speak with the polite curtness he always had employed towards his deputy.

Alone once more the Baron could mop his face again, with the handkerchief that was more than damp. The heat was dreadful. So was the strain. And time had fled by on wings; now it was past five o'clock on a glaring, brassy evening.

The telephone buzzed on his desk, and he picked it up. "Major Schimpf is asking for orders, sir," said Fink's voice.

"Who is he?"

"Chief of Staff to General Keil, sir."

Keil of the 98th Armored, the division which the Count had asked him to route through Berlin today.

"What does he want?" asked the Baron desperately.

"You had better speak to him yourself, sir," said Fink; he bleated the helpless reply like an old sheep. Yet even though he bleated, he acted; there was a click as the connection was transferred before the Baron could say more.

"What is it, Schimpf?" demanded the Baron as brusquely as he could manage.

"I am asking for confirmation of my orders, sir," said a voice in the well-trained accent of the General Staff.

"What are they?"

"They reroute the division via Berlin, sir."

"Where are you?"

"Wittenberge, sir. The general and I arrived by road and found these orders awaiting us by teletype."

"Where's your division?"

"The first train is due in half an hour."

"And who signs these orders?"

"Chief of Staff, Home Army, sir."

"Ah!" The Baron tried to make the monosyllable completely expressionless.

"It's a clear-the-road order," said Schimpf. "First priority."

That order, if obeyed, would bring the first echelon of the 98th into Berlin two hours from leaving Wittenberge. The whole division could be detrained and ready for action in the city—unless an Allied air raid imposed delay—before midnight. And only a few minutes ago the Baron had been congratulating himself that so far all his actions had been strictly correct. Now he was faced with the immediate necessity of taking sides, and Fink was listening on the extension. No! It was not quite an immediate necessity.

"Your first train due in half an hour, you say?"

"Yes, sir."

"I'll confirm or countermand those orders within that time," said the Baron, trying to pick his words with all the care he could. "Telephone again five minutes before your first train is due."

"But sir! The priority—"

"That will do, Schimpf," said the Baron harshly, putting down the receiver.

The existence of a clear-the-road order between Wittenberge and Berlin would play havoc with the orderly flow of traffic. If it were going to be countermanded it should be done at once. Yet— What was he to say in twenty-five minutes from now?

The door opened to the sound of music. Light dance music! Fink was carrying in a portable radio.

Indecision 117

"An announcement, sir," he said. "The minister—Goebbels himself."

"Very well."

Fink put the instrument down on the desk, and the two of them looked at it as it ground out a frivolous tune; it might have been a ticking bomb. The reddening sunlight was pouring in through the windows. The music stopped in the middle of a bar, and an expressionless voice announced the Minister for Public Enlightenment. There was no mistaking Goebbels's voice following immediately after, that excellent speaking voice, impassioned or sarcastic, serious or sad at will. He wasted no time in getting to the heart of the matter.

"An attempt has been made on the life of our Fuehrer. He was very slightly injured, although several of his personal staff were killed or mortally wounded. His slight injury has in no way interrupted his performance of his onerous duties, and he is at present in conference with *il Duce*, Signor Mussolini, our devoted ally, who arrived at Fuehrer Headquarters immediately after the dastardly attempt. The Fuehrer will address his devoted people over the radio tonight at midnight, when we will all be able to listen to his beloved voice and will be able to renew our vows of eternal allegiance to Fuehrer, Race, and Reich. Our hearts go out to him in this solemn moment when we know that Providence has guarded him from a great danger, and we can rejoice to know that the dastardly attempt was the work only of a small group of disloyal officers of the General Staff, seduced from their allegiance by International Jewry. Now there can be an end to the rumors which the Jewish agents are

circulating. We can all remain tranquil and loyal, paying no attention to any further attempts by International
Jewry to disturb our peace and our allegiance, while we
wait to hear that voice which we all know and love. We
can all say, deep in our hearts, *'Heil Hitler! Sieg Heil!
Sieg Heil!'* "

The blare of a band bursting into the Horst Wessel
song followed instantly on Goebbels's last words, and
the Baron and Fink were left, as so often before, looking
at each other. Neither dared say a word, but the Baron's
brain was hard at work. Undoubtedly that was Goebbels's voice. But if the Fuehrer were dead or under arrest
Goebbels would be saying just the same things, playing
for time while the Nazis gathered their forces to strike
back at the army; it might be significant that the Fuehrer was delaying his broadcast until midnight, but then
it might not. With Mussolini on his hands and with the
most important speech of his life to prepare, Hitler
might well need time. Only one thing was certain, and
that was that the Nazis still had possession of the broadcasting station; it might be significant or it might not.
Thank God he still had not committed himself, although—the Baron looked at the clock—the minutes
were now flying by.

The radio was still blaring, and suddenly through its
din another noise was to be heard, a rumbling and roaring down below in the street, which until now had been
so quiet. The Baron hurried to the window; Fink
snapped off the radio and followed him. A long column
of trucks and lorries was rolling along the street towards
the Bendlerstrasse; looking down onto each, the Baron
saw steel helmets, packed close together; the trucks were

full of troops. At the machine guns mounted over the cabs and pointing out from behind were soldiers, braced and ready to fire. Soldiers! Not police, not SS, but soldiers!

"Wachtbataillon Grossdeutchland," said Fink, reading the badges.

"Brought in from Doeberitz, then," said the Baron. It was one of the best of the battalions of guards, but the Baron had no knowledge as to who was its commanding officer. It occured to him at that moment that if he had fallen in with the Count's suggestion it would not be one battalion in trucks, but Keil's whole division in tanks that would now be rumbling down the street. If—he looked at the clock again—in ten minutes' time he confirmed the Home Army's orders Keil would be here by midnight. It was desperately important to know if the battalion was acting under the orders of a living Hitler, or of a Goebbels fighting for his life with Hitler dead, or of von Witzleben the self-appointed Commander in Chief. Torture chambers and firing parties. The last truck in the column had vanished from sight now, round the corner to the Bendlerstrasse, and all was deathly quiet again. Time was passing. Torture chambers and firing parties! And then, clear and loud through the sultry stillness, came the sound of a volley, rifle fire, half a dozen rifles fired not quite at the same moment. That was a firing squad, an execution, in the Bendlerstrasse. The Baron started to look over at Fink and then changed his mind, he could not trust himself to meet anyone's eyes, and he looked at the ceiling instead. Now another volley. The sweat inside the Baron's shirt was icy cold. It was hard to think. Who was shooting whom? Was von Witzleben making an example of officers who had not come over wholeheartedly to his side? Another volley. Who had died then? Some SS spy or some friend on the General Staff? God, another volley! There was a massacre going on.

A massacre! That settled it. Von Witzleben would not order a massacre in the Bendlerstrasse. If von Witzleben were in power there might well be a massacre at Goebbels's house in the Herman Goeringstrasse, or at the Gestapo Headquarters in the Prinz Albrechtstrasse, but not here. There was another volley, and another. Victims must be being dragged in rapid succession before the firing squads. Loud, shattering reports, announcing to the waiting city that order was being restored. There could be no doubt about it. Thank God he had not committed himself on the wrong side. Time was just up.

"Colonel Fink!"

"Sir!" Fink's heels came together with a click, his hands at the seams of his trousers.

"Telephone immediately to Fuehrer Headquarters. Tell them that the 98th Armored is entrained at Wittenberge ready for immediate transfer to Berlin if they think it necessary."

"Very well, sir."

Now the Baron could meet Fink's eyes with a steady glance. But as Fink put out his hand to open the door it opened to admit three SS officers, pistols in their hands.

"You are under arrest," said the leader, and the Baron submitted to arrest with an easy mind; it would not take long to clear himself.

"And why did you plot with the Count?" asked the Gestapo officer for the twentieth time.

"I did not! I did not!" said the Baron. "I swear it!"

The Gestapo officer nodded to one of his assistants, who opened the door of the cell and gave an order. Two hard-faced young men came in, dragging between them a wreck of a man, shrinking yet helpless. It was hard to recognize him as Fink. The two hard-faced young men propped him up between them, to face the Baron and the Gestapo officer.

"Did the Count come to call on the Baron in his office on the eighteenth?" asked the latter.

"Yes—oh yes!" said Fink.

"You saw them together?"

"Yes!"

"Did they look like conspirators? Did they?"

"Yes!"

"You interrupted them conspiring?"

"Yes!"

Fink had come in to find them both adjusting their monocles—Oh God! The Baron remembered thinking that it might well have been a secret sign.

"Did the Count say anything as he left?"

"Yes!"

"What was it?"

Fink's pale gray eyes could not focus; they seemed to be unseeing as they passed over the Baron's face.

"What was it?"

"He said—he said—'Remember what I said,' he said!"

"Now, Baron, what was it the Count had said?"

"But I didn't do it! I didn't do it! You can look at the orders."

"What was it he asked you to do?"

The Count was dead, shot in the courtyard at the Bendlerstrasse. He could not be hurt further, not like the Baron. The Baron told, spluttering, about the Count's request to route the 98th Armored through Berlin.

"But I didn't do it. You can tell I didn't do it! I routed them through Wittenberge."

"So? Did it not occur to you, Baron, that one telephone call to Fuehrer Headquarters, or to Gestapo Headquarters here, would have nipped the conspiracy in the bud? Was it not your duty to make that call?"

The Baron swallowed hard. To his credit it simply had not occurred to him that he might have betrayed his friends. Surprise delayed his answer, which should have been pat enough.

"But that wasn't the reason I was asked. It was because—"

The Baron rambled on explaining the personal relationships between Keil and Sepp Dietrich and Geyr von Schweppenburg.

"Send a message to France to have General Keil arrested wherever he is, at the front or anywhere else," said the Gestapo officer to an assistant, and then he turned back to the Baron. "Now why did you hesitate before you answered my question, Baron?"

The questioning went on. All the pettinesses, all the shiftinesses, were revealed. Schimpf had telephoned from Wittenberge. Why had he not instantly been told that all orders from the Bendlerstrasse had been countermanded by Fuehrer Headquarters? Why that delay? Why? Why? Why? And Stauffenberg, the man who had tried to blow up the Fuehrer, the man who had flown back to rouse

Berlin to rebellion, was a cousin of the Baron's. Was that not so?

"No!"

The Gestapo officer referred to a notebook.

"There was a marriage in 1878," he said, "between a Countess von Stauffenberg and—"

That was the Baron's great-uncle.

"I never thought about that for one moment," said the Baron.

No? And what about the Baron's membership in the Herrenklub? And what about—? The true and the partly true and the false, the relevant and the irrelevant —the latter strangely transmuted into matters of great importance—all were worked in together.

"No need for further questioning," said the Gestapo officer at length, in a patronizing tone. All his contempt for blue blood, for great mental powers, was evident in his words. These pitiful gentlemen of the General Staff who could not construct a watertight conspiracy!

"You will appear before the Court of Honor tomorrow," said the Gestapo officer, and the Baron looked at him stupidly. His emotions were all exhausted now. There was nothing left in him. And yet his mind was still ticking over slowly. The Court of Honor would cast him out of the army, so that the People's Court that would follow would not suffer the pain of finding an army officer guilty of treason. The People's Court—a blaring judge, a jeering prosecution, an inevitable sentence, and then a slow hanging. He could have made that telephone call and betrayed his friends, or he could have brought the 98th Armored up to Berlin; but he had done neither.

THE HEAD AND THE FEET

Georg Schmidt was not happy in his job as medical officer of the Rosenberg concentration camp. There were many days when he regretted, when he sorrowed deeply over, his initial weaknesses which had given the SS the hint that he was a suitable and pliable instrument for them. Now he was in their clutches and there was no way out for him—the only possible way, that of volunteering for active service with the Waffen SS in the field, was barred by reason of his advanced age. Schmidt often remembered the brutal speech of an SS officer to a newly arrived batch of prisoners.

"You are here to work, and work you shall. For the man who cannot work, and for the man who will not work, there is the gas chamber. Work or death—there is no other future for you."

There was no other future for Schmidt, either, and he knew it well. Nor could he ever allow the world a glimpse of his feelings; they must always be concealed. The SS was proud of the intensity of its patriotism and of the fervor of its faith in National Socialism, and it would never tolerate the existence of a halfhearted member. The knowledge made Schmidt's situation all the

worse, for it deprived him of any pleasure in getting
drunk; in alcoholic stupor he could be oblivious of his
troubles, but while he was achieving that condition he
was always gnawed at by the thought of what he might
blurt out before he was quite drunk, and the cold fears
that thought aroused poisoned his liquor and delayed its
action, so that he would sometimes spend the evening in
his quarters, unable to get drunk, yammering to himself
in a nightmare of misery. The world thinks of the men
who staffed the concentration camps as fiends of hell;
fiends they were, but they were in hell too, some of them.

That was not true of Sturmbannfuehrer Schiller, the
camp commandant, who was a man without humour or
moods, whose conscience was in the keeping of the SS,
and who was actuated by no motives beyond a mild
personal ambition and a desire to carry out to the letter
the orders of higher authority. As long as Headquarters
at Oranienburg couched the order in the proper form,
and it bore the correct signature, Sturmbannfuehrer
Schiller would have pushed his own mother into the
gas chamber without a moment's hesitation or regret,
Schmidt thought. The two men were together in the
commandant's office; Schmidt had just made his report
after his morning rounds, and had laid stress on the necessity for temporary isolation and thorough delousing
of a new batch of Ruthenians who had just arrived; he
suspected they had brought typhus with them.

"I have made a note of it," said Schiller. "Meanwhile
there is a question of some other arrivals beside the
Ruthenians."

"Yes, Commandant," said Schmidt.

He knew perfectly well there had been some other arrivals, and so did all the rest of the staff, and probably the prisoners as well, but as there had been ostentatious secrecy about the matter he judged it best to make a show of ignorance. But during the night a small amount of motor transport had arrived, conveying a number of new SS troopers and presumably some other people, for one of the detached huts on the perimeter of the camp was now guarded by sentries with new faces, and foot traffic along the path leading past it was now prohibited.

"There are four new prisoners in Block 11," explained Schiller. "They have been sent here with their papers marked for 'special treatment!' "

"I understand, Commandant," said Schmidt.

He knew those fatal words well. The prisoner whose papers bore them—*besondere Behandlung*— was marked by Oranienburg for execution. Death stalked about Rosenberg camp in many forms. Death in the gas chamber —that was of every-day occurrence; death under the whips and rifle butts of the guards; death from disease and privation; death from suicide. But "special treatment" meant something far more formal and far less casual than all those; it meant capital punishment carried out with the ritual and elaboration of the old days when execution only followed murder. It meant a fixed time and place, the presence of witnesses, the signing of certificates, even if the methods of execution were sometimes strange and even if the whole affair was shrouded in secrecy. Now and then there would be public and formal hangings, carried out on the central parade ground in sight of all the mustered prisoners—that would be when some prisoner had been guilty of sabotage, or insubordination, or attempted escape. Sometimes there would be private hangings, in a little hut at the back of the crematorium to which the bodies would be speedily and secretly transferred; there was a row of hooks in a beam in that hut, and lengths of supple rope kept ready, and a heavy bench from which the victims could be pushed. Who those victims were, and why they were accorded this particular "special treatment," their crimes and the reasons for secrecy, were matters with which only Headquarters were concerned, and it would be better if no one else were to inquire into them.

There had been two victims—both women—who had had very special treatment indeed; at Schiller's orders Schmidt had told them that they were to be inoculated against typhus, and Schmidt had injected subcutaneously so large a dose of morphine that they had slipped away into final unconsciousness without any of the bitterness of death. But on the other hand there had been some men who had been slowly strangled—slowly, and with many intermissions—while an official photographer had recorded the process for the subsequent delectation of some unknown but certainly lofty official, perhaps the same one whose softheartedness had selected the fate of the women.

So with all these possibilities Schmidt had to await further instructions from Schiller.

"The special treatment indicated by the orders I have received," said Schmidt, "is decapitation."

Schmidt knew he should answer "Yes, Commandant" as always, but this time the words would not come, for he was surprised, even though seven years of service in a concentration camp should have rendered him immune to surprise. But Schiller waited patiently for his reply, and he made it at last. He should not have been surprised, for a very early decree by the Fuehrer years ago, had re-established decapitation as a method of punishment in the Reich.

"The headsman," went on Schiller, "is here. He was brought by the same convoy as brought the prisoners. He is under confinement too, to make sure he will be sober when the time comes."

"And when is the time?" asked Schmidt, knowing the question was expected of him.

Schiller tapped thoughtfully on his desk with the butt of his pen. The length of four human lives was being determined by his decision, but Schiller really did not give a thought to that. If he named an early hour in the morning his wife would be distressed at having to rise unusually early to sit with him at breakfast, but if he left it until later his necessary attendance at the function would break into his comfortable morning routine of correspondence and reports. But it would be best to get it over before the camp was roused at dawn, because otherwise the prisoners with their lively powers of observation would perhaps guess what was going on. He made a compromise decision.

"Five-thirty," he said, at length. "You will be present from five-fifteen."

"Very well, Commandant," said Schmidt.

"The certificates must be prepared immediately after the execution," added Schiller. "The escort will leave as soon as cremation is complete and the officer in command is to take them with him."

"Very well," said Schmidt.

Even he, even in his present mood, quite failed to see

anything odd about the regulations that made it necessary to have a qualified medical man in attendance to
certify the cause of death when men were going to have
their heads severed from their bodies; routine, regulations, precedents all demanded his presence, and it did
not occur to him to revolt against them—not that he
would have done so, in any case, naturally.

"I will see you there," said Schiller. "Heil Hitler!"

"Heil Hitler!" said Schmidt.

At five o'clock in the morning, when Schmidt was
called, it was still perfectly dark and shuddering cold.
He huddled himself into his uniform and drank a hurried cup of coffee—even at this stage of the war coffee
was the only unsatisfactory ration allotted to the SS—
and walked across the parade ground from his quarters. A few shaded lamps threw beams of light along the
fences of barbed wire, so that the guards in the towers
had the whole perimeter under observation. The whole
camp was deadly quiet, even though five thousand men
and women lay there in confinement. He saw a sudden
gleam of flame from the chimney of the crematorium; a
Kapo was firing it up in readiness. But there was no one
near the little shed with the beam and the hooks.
Schmidt realized that of course there would not be room
enough there for the swing of an ax, and in a sudden
fear lest he should be late he hurried on to where light
from an opening door revealed dark figures moving
about. He arrived a little short of breath, and only just
in time, at the vacant shed near the guardhouse. Schiller
was just entering, his adjutant with him.

"Heil Hitler!" said Schmidt, saluting.

"Heil Hitler!" grunted Schiller, who was never at his best early in the morning.

Preparations had already been made in the shed. The floor boards—if there ever had been any—had been removed to reveal the naked earth, and in the middle of the shed stood a large cube of wood; dangling over the cube, illuminating it starkly against the sawdust, hung a bright electric lamp. Schiller and Schmidt and the adjutant took their positions beside the block, and as they did so three more men came in through the door. They all wore leather aprons, but one of them was bare to the waist despite the cold. He was a man of immense physique, something under thirty, bulging with muscle, and he carried the largest ax that Schmidt had ever seen; along the edge it certainly measured sixteen inches, and it was clear, from the way the big man handled it, that the huge head weighed several pounds. Schmidt found himself thinking that the ax head would do the job of its own weight, but he next decided that it would be all the more necessary to have a powerful man to wield it, to swing it up and bring it down. The executioner took his place by the block; he measured his distance from it with his eye, lifted the ax to it, bending his knees and shifting his feet until he was satisfied with his position, like a golfer addressing his ball. At length he stood erect, the ax head resting by his feet, and the helve in his hands, and then in came an SS officer and two SS men with the first victim. He was frightened. He dragged his feet and he moaned pitifully, but not for long.

"Next!" called the officer—hardly necessary after that loud thump. And then again, after the ax had once more swung slowly up and come hurtling down, "Next!"

Schmidt found he had to look away. He shifted his position a little, and holding himself at attention with his eyes looking straight before him, he could direct his rigid stare away from what was going on, even though he could not close his ears to it. Nor could he numb his sensation of touch. Immediately after the next thump he heard something bounce in front of him, and he felt something bump against his feet, and he looked down with something of horror at what had struck him, until one of the men in the leather aprons stooped and lifted it away.

"Next!" said the SS officer.

The horror grew inside Schmidt as he thought again of what had bumped against his feet. He was shuddering and felt sick, so that this time he paid no attention to what was going on and was only recalled to reality by the clear expressionless voice of the SS officer.

"So perish all enemies of the Reich! Heil Hitler!"

"Heil Hitler!" chorused most of those present—most of those present who were still alive—and then Schiller turned to Schmidt.

"The certificates are in my office. Please come and sign them."

When Schmidt straightened himself up from the desk, recapping his fountain pen, Schiller had an invitation for him.

"Next Wednesday is my birthday," he said, with a smile. "I hope you will come to a party at my house. A little wine—a little coffee—at four o'clock? Next Wednesday?"

"Of course, I shall be delighted," said Schmidt.

It was an effort to smile and bow; Schmidt was sure he must be looking white and sick—he could still feel that thing bumping against his feet, so that it was all he could do not to look down at his boots.

"Excellent! My wife will be pleased," said Schiller, and then in dismissal, "Heil Hitler!"

Outside it was still quite dark, only the barest hint of dawn in the east, but a gush of flames flared up again from the chimney of the crematorium. By the guard-house stood the trucks which were to take the SS men away to their next duty. Two dark figures were lifting a heavy cube up into one of the trucks. And in the darkness, as he walked along, Schmidt could still feel the sensation of that bump against his feet.

It was strange how it still lingered with him. He went back to his quarters, stripped, and stood under the shower and scrubbed his feet, telling himself at the same time that it was quite absurd that he should do so, for he had been wearing his uniform boots when it had happened and it was impossible that he should be polluted, that anything could have infected him. But when, dressed again, he went over to the mess and sat down to the breakfast, he bumped his foot against the table leg, not hard, almost gently, the way—the way his foot had been bumped before. The result was that he snarled at the morning greetings of his brother officers ungraciously enough to make the adjutant cock an eye at him; part of the oath of the SS was to swear true comradeship with all one's fellow members and Schmidt's behavior was therefore suspicious.

Schmidt's upset temper continued. At the sick parade he was testy and curt. Today he did not draw even his usual consolation from the fact that he never had to combat malingering; the prison sick always did their pathetic best to appear as well as possible, for they knew that the gas chamber awaited the seriously ill. The man today whom he ordered to the hospital actually begged not to be sent; he dropped on his knees—he was an oldish man of no spirit—and tried to grasp the skirt of Schmidt's tunic in supplication, and when Schmidt drew back he overbalanced forward and grasped at Schmidt's feet, provoking a burst of wrath which took Schmidt's assistants by surprise, as he was usually even-tempered; they sought to please him (they were all Kapos—hated by their fellow prisoners and despised by their masters) by beating the old man with their sticks as they dragged him away. But after Schmidt had completed his morning duties he went under the shower again, as he usually did, and he found himself scrubbing his feet again. He remembered that bump against them so well; the memory kept on returning to him.

He could not lose that memory, however much he tried; there were little incidents all through the day that brought it back to him, a touch here, a bump there. He found himself, when he wanted to put on his slippers, actually shrinking from putting his hands to his boots, and when he drank his fourth glass of schnapps he suddenly leaped up from his chair, shaking, for he was sure he had felt something strike against his feet again. It was the same when he went to bed; he composed himself for sleep, and he drifted off, stupefied, and then woke instantly with a start, sweating, his heart thumping, for he had dreamed in those few seconds of sleep that something had struck against his feet. He hated his feet, down there at the far end of the bed. Muzzy with drink and yet at the same time tense and nervous he had to get up and stagger over to the dispensary for a drug to induce sleep, and then that was worse, for the drug seemed to bind and shackle him in his dreams, holding him helpless while Things—not well-defined Things, but Things with eyes and mouths—bounced and touched his feet.

Next morning, standing by his bed with his hand on his dressing table to steady himself, he addressed himself seriously, as seriously as his aching head would permit. This was all nonsense. He would be going insane if he allowed this to go on. After all he had seen and endured it was absurd to allow one single petty incident to upset him in this fashion. He must put it out of his mind altogether. He must not shudder like that at the recollection of his dreams. Nor must he step aside hastily as he had just done at the thought of Things touching his feet. No, he must not. He had a professional familiarity with insanity, naturally, and he knew about the growth of delusions; he had seen delusions of touch before. But in the shower it was hard not to stoop down with the scrubbing brush and scrub and scrub at his feet in the hope of abolishing the feeling of a cold poison upon their skin. Did a snake have saliva? The cold saliva of a snake was the idea in his mind at the moment. Absurd, of course—that had no relation at all to—to what had actually happened. He swore violently.

In the mess the adjutant cocked an eye at him again, noting the imperfect shave and the dirty handkerchief. They were affronts to the tradition of the SS, which demanded the most careful, ritual bodily cleanliness. The adjutant had to think about his duty, for he was a member of a very special body, of the police within the police. Juvenal had asked, eighteen hundred years earlier, "Who shall guard the guards?" and Himmler had found the answer to that question; the adjutant was one of those people who reported to Himmler on the people who reported to Himmler. Schmidt was aware of the glance the adjutant shot at him, and his condition was not bettered on that account. It made him concerned about his feet again. He dragged the polluted things about with him all day as he did his day's duty, most painfully conscious of them, and the night was even worse. The delusions were out of control altogether now; they had fastened upon him and could not let go. Rosenberg concentration camp was a hell-pit of despair and misery, and the camp doctor now had his share too. His word could deal out death—and it did, hundreds of times—and the prisoners in their profound misery did their best to flatter him, to please him, to gain his favor. They cringed to him like beaten dogs, while he walked among them on a pair of feet that he believed to be spongy and rotten with poison; feet that, whenever his attention was diverted, might be bumped against by Things. There were days of this life, days and days— and nights and nights.

Then came the commandant's birthday, to be celebrated with all the sentiment of the German tradition, and Schmidt made a serious effort to pull himself together for the occasion. He shaved a second time, even though it was only early afternoon, trying to smile with sympathy at the haggard old face that looked back at him from the mirror. He had his clothes most carefully brushed, and he was proud of himself for being able to

order without a quaver a special polishing of his boots
without a thought of—of what he must not think about.
He must not think about his feet as they went one-two
one-two when he marched out through the prison gate;
the SS were always smart and military in appearance
and movement, and though he was middle-aged he
could be as smart and military as the spotless sentry at
the gate who saluted him. Smart and upright even with
feet that—that—; no, he must not think about his feet.

The commandant lived a domestic life in the bosom
of his family during the hours when he was not engaged
on the business of the state in Rosenberg concentration
camp. He had taken a little house in the village a mile
from the gate, where he dwelt with his wife and children, happily uxorious, indulgent to his children, and
polite to his neighbors despite his rank, although they
could not forget the dreaded uniform he wore, while
they tried to be ignorant of what happened behind the
barbed wire fences of the camp a mile up the road which
they never walked along. The commandant was a good
host now; he made Schmidt welcome, and received his
felicitations on his birthday with delighted modesty.
Schmidt bowed over Frau Sturmbannfuehrer Schiller's
hand and told her that every day she looked younger
and more charming. He bowed to his brother officers—
the adjutant was there, of course—and he made himself
agreeable to their wives. Five of the officers had been
fortunate enough to be able to establish their wives in
the village, and they and their wives and a couple of
other officers from the camp constituted the party, no
one else. The black uniforms lived in isolation; they saw
each other every day, but for this occasion they made

polite conversation as if they had not met for weeks, and they talked to the wives, and the wives talked to them, as if they were people of normal life, as if the hideous cruelty in which they dealt daily had never been thought of.

What went on in the concentration camp was supposed to be kept secret and never described in the outside world, but perhaps husbands talked to wives; perhaps those wives knew, as they talked to their husbands' colleagues, what frightful deeds of blood those colleagues had perpetrated, but they showed no sign of it. They smiled and they discussed airy nothings; perhaps as a butcher's wife will talk with another butcher. And the children, when they were brought into the party, in their best clothes and with their hair tidy, were cooed over and complimented. The five-year-old and the three-year-old bobbed and curtsied as they were told, but little Hildegard was only one and a half, and when she was put down on the floor she escaped from her mother with a gurgle of glee and ran with unsteady steps and outspread arms into the crowded room. Schmidt drew hastily back to avoid her clutch round his legs—he did not want his feet touched as the hospital patient had touched them—and she fell with a bump on her nose at his feet and wailed in consequence. The women looked their disapprobation at Schmidt for allowing it to happen, but he was only an old widower, after all, and had had nothing to do with children, so they decided he was to be pitied rather than to be condemned. But the adjutant saw and was not so lenient in his judgment, for kindness to children and animals should be, as the SS doctrine laid down, characteristic of a member of the SS.

It was even worse ten minutes later, just when Schmidt was talking again to Frau Neumann and priding himself on behaving naturally. Something bumped against his feet, something solid. Frau Neumann saw the expression of his face change, saw the horror in it. The wine in the glass that Schmidt held was jerked out in a golden arc as he kicked out wildly. There was a sharp yelp, and everyone looked down and round to see Sturmbannfuehrer Schiller's little dachshund, which had managed to make its way into the room when the children were taken out, proclaiming the sorrow of an affectionate advance being received by a kick in the ribs. There was more reproach in the eyes of the women as they looked at Schmidt, but he was hardly aware of it, with the sweat standing out on his forehead and his hands shaking.

Schmidt was the first guest to leave that party, even though the sane part of his mind told him that perhaps it was a little unwise to do so. The others would be given an opportunity to discuss him and his peculiarities. He was not, in any case, a man who enjoyed the company of other people; moreover, although the sane part of his mind told him, too, that he should stay here amid the lights and the distractions, the insane part wanted to take him away like a wounded animal, into darkness and solitude. The sane part of his mind made him shake Sturmbannfuehrer Schiller's hand politely and renew his congratulations on the anniversary, and made him thank Frau Sturmbannfuehrer Schiller for a magnificent party, but the insane part asserted itself again as he walked in the darkness back to the camp.

A strange suggestion was making itself felt in his

mind. These feet, these horrible feet of his, might be got rid of. He pictured himself lying on his back in his bed, revolver in hand, taking aim at those feet and shooting them off, bit by bit. There was something strangely tempting in the idea; it would mean the end of his troubles. But what was left of his sanity asserted itself again and argued with his insanity. It would be painful (but was not that really an argument in its favor?), and it would be impractical (but perhaps not to a man as filled with an inward spirit as he was), and it was the insane who practiced horrible mutilations upon themselves (but the insane did not have the justification he had—they had not had his experience), and he would feel better in the morning (but before morning he had still to go through the night).

As he plodded on up the road to the camp the arguments presented by his sanity fought a losing battle with those presented by his insanity. By the time he had reached the gate he was thinking about his project with something of warm anticipation. He would free himself from his disgusting feet; he had practically decided upon it as he stood by the gate for the sergeant of the guard to identify him—he was even a little afraid lest the sergeant should read his intention in his expression and prevent him for some reason.

That started another train of thought as he walked into the dark camp. The SS would look upon his act as self-mutilation to avoid duty. Then he would be misunderstood—that was the trouble, not the fear of what would be done to the remainder of him in that event. He did not like that thought, and he felt bitter disappointment at having to give up the project. He stamped with his disgusting feet in rage as he walked along through the camp.

There, hardly visible in the darkness, was the shed where—where it had happened. There was the gas chamber which had so often held the heaped up dead. There was the private execution shed with its beam and its hooks and its supple ropes with running nooses. A new idea struck him, one which was not disapproved by any part of his mind. He walked in the darkness to the shed; even in the deeper darkness within it he could find his way about, feel for a hook and a rope, climb up onto the bench. This was gratifying; this was an ingenious way round the difficulties which no one less clever than he could have thought of. There was something wayward and pixielike in his mood now in his moment of triumph. It was that which made him say "Heil Hitler!" before he stepped off the bench.

THE UNBELIEVABLE

Outside the dockyard gate the crowd had become denser and denser. The first-comers, on their arrival, had spread themselves out thinly, each family group reserving to itself a sufficient space of snow-covered ground to give themselves ample room in which to sit, or to lie, and even, for the fortunate ones who had food and fuel, to light little fires for warmth and for cooking, among the railway tracks of the vast marshaling yard that lay between the dockyard and the city. But now the thousands, the scores of thousands, of people who had arrived had pressed towards the dockyard gate, thicker and thicker, so that anyone who ventured to sit down in the filthy and tramped snow ran the risk of being trodden into it, so that it was necessary to stand up all the time, through the day and through the night, until one's knees gave away with weariness and one fell underfoot. It was bad for the children, for the aged, and for the invalids, who still formed a fair proportion of the crowd even though so many had been weeded out in the course of the long flight from the Russians.

That dockyard gate, lofty and with the ornate ugliness of a happier age, marked the farthest limit of the flight. The crowd could go no farther; the pressure of a hundred thousand people might well have beat in its sturdy iron bars had it not been for the sentries within, who stood with Tommy guns in their hands, anxious and determined, looking out through the bars at the silent crowd. Their orders were of the strictest; at any attempt to storm the gate they were to open fire instantly, without waiting for any further word, and at that time and in that place orders had to be obeyed, so that the young men in their naval greatcoats kept their gloved fingers ready on their triggers to fire on the women and the children and the old men, on the women who might be their mothers and the men who might be their fathers.

They were fine young men, these men in naval uniforms, the cream of what was left of Germany, of perfect physique and of stolid temperament, for they were the latest recruits for the submarine service, undergoing —until being set to guard the gate—their final training before going out underwater to maintain the U-boat campaign. They were the men who (as a few optimists still hoped) might win the war for the Reich by the aid of the secret weapons Dr. Goebbels hinted at. But now the U-boat campaign would be interrupted, because the flood of Russian invasion was racing along the Baltic coast, and one base after another was falling into Russian hands; for five years the Swastika flag had flown unchallenged over the Baltic and a thousand U-boats and their crews had exercised there, working up to the perfection of technique, ready for the assault on the Anglo-Saxon shipping. The five years were at an end now; control of the Baltic was slipping out of German hands not as the result of any naval defeat there but be-

cause of something even more utterly incredible—the
advance of the Red armies to capture the bases from the
land side. They were no more than ten miles from the
dockyard gate at this very moment; a thin desperate cordon of German troops was endeavoring to hold them
back, and the whole ten-mile strip of land, from the
dockyard gate to the immediate back areas of the fighting line, was filled with refugees from the eastern
provinces, jammed between the Russians and the water's
edge, between the devil and the deep sea. The cold, pen-
etrating wind that blew from the east brought with it
the sound of the artillery fire.

A platoon of armed men came marching through the
vast crowd. It had to cleave its way like a ship through
the sea, and its progress, just like that of a ship, was
marked by two long spreading ripples on either side as
heads were turned towards them—or away; those men
wore the black trappings of dread and there were many
among the crowd who wished to attract no attention
from the SS. The Obersturmfuehrer—lieutenant—in
command suddenly stopped and pointed into the crowd.

"You!" he said.

The man to whom he pointed was obviously young;
the thick stubble on his face was of a light brown. He
wavered before the pointing finger, and then braced
himself to answer boldly.

"Sir!" he said, in a tone of perfect innocence; but that
momentary wavering had betrayed him.

"Come here," said the Obersturmfuehrer. "Come!"

The man's glance strayed from side to side, but flight
was hopeless, and again he made himself appear quite
composed as he came through the crowd; the crowd

parted hastily to make way for him, as if he had some horrible contagion, but a woman, bundled into a man's heavy civilian greatcoat, followed at his heels. The man stood at attention before the Obersturmfuehrer; he had only one hand to put to the seam of his trousers; his right sleeve was empty and pinned up into his armpit.

"Who are you?" snapped the SS officer.

"Schenk, sir. Ludwig Karl. Gefreiter, 118th Artillery, discharged. Born at Schleppe, Border Province, 1907. Got this at Smolensk in '41. Settled on a farm at Bielsk under the Scheme."

"Papers?"

"None, sir," said Schenk deprecatingly. "Left in a hurry."

"So?" said the officer.

There was nothing specially remarkable about the man having no papers. And a man with one arm had little need to prove he was useless for combat. That was the point. And why that shifty look when he had first been addressed?

"Turn round," said the officer.

Schenk hesitated perceptibly; that might be a flicker of fear in his eyes.

Schenk obeyed reluctantly, and the officer eyed his back while the woman uttered a low moan. It was the moan that settled it; the slightly misshapen appearance of the man's back might not have called for action.

"Take off his coat!" ordered the officer to the two men nearest him. Schenk struggled for a moment, unavailingly. One greatcoat and then a second were torn from him, and then his jacket. His villainy was revealed.

He still had his right arm. He had bent it up behind his back under his shirt.

"So!" said the officer again, but not in a musing manner this time. The woman was shrieking.

The officer looked round about him. Close to the dockyard gate was a little beerhouse, shuttered and apparently empty now. In front of it stood wooden tables and some benches, over which stretched a wooden framework which had once supported an awning; under the awning in sunny and happy days dockyard workers had once sat to drink their beer. Now the terrace was occupied by refugees; old men were sitting, dozing on the benches, and weary mothers had rested their babies on their bundles on the tables.

"That will do," said the Obersturmfuehrer. "Bring him along."

The man cried out and struggled; the woman screamed. The almost senseless words she uttered yet revealed a terrible truth. She was not speaking German but Polish; the deserter was guilty of a further crime; he had been cohabiting with a Slavic woman, one of an inferior race.

"Bring her too," said the Obersturmfuehrer.

The SS men dragged the pair through the crowd, which huddled together to make a lane for their passage. They reached the beerhouse.

"Clear out!" snapped the Obersturmfuehrer to the people huddled there. "Clear out!"

It only called for that single repetition of the order to penetrate the numbed minds of the refugees. Wearily they gathered up their possessions; women led their ex-

hausted fathers and fathers-in-law away—one woman
had actually to unfasten an old man from the bench to
which she had tied his arm, for, far advanced in senility
and yet not physically disabled, he was liable to wander
away while she attended to her children. The SS men
swept them all from the terrace, forcing them away to
crowd in among the already crowded refugees at the
gate; they had to push and squeeze to make their way,
because those already in position made no voluntary
move to accommodate them; some were numb with
misery and others were staring fascinated at the preparations made by the SS men, while a few of the women
hid their eyes or tried to close their ears to the shrieks
the deserter was still hurling into the pitiless wind. The
little children looked on solemnly as if with grave understanding.

The Obersturmfuehrer was a man of few words. He
made a sweeping gesture to his men, which took in the
tables, the beams overhead, and the wires of the dangling electric lights; from the smooth efficiency with
which the men worked it seemed as if they did not need
even that small amount of direction. One of them leaped
onto a table and cut a wire loose and swung it over one
of the beams.

The Obersturmfuehrer was already giving his attention to the next step of his plan. He eyed the cardboard
advertisements that hung beside the shutters of the beerhouse; he went up to them and found, to his satisfaction, that the back of each was blank and smooth and
offered a fair surface on which to write. With it in his
hand he walked over to one of the little fires a family
was maintaining, and selected a burning stick from it,

which he extinguished in the snow. With the charred end he was able to write, crudely but boldly and legibly on the back, just a brief message in huge capitals—I DESERTED. He had hardly finished the writing when the last shriek of the deserter ended in a horrible sound as they thrust him from the table. The Obersturmfuehrer handed the notice to one of the men.

"Hang it on his chest," he said.

Then he jerked his thumb at the Polish woman, and turned away to take down a second advertisement. On the back of this one he wrote another message—I HELPED HIM.

When it was all over he condescended to address himself to his subordinate officer, Untersturmfuehrer Voss.

"That will be a good lesson," he said.

"No doubt," said Voss, in a thin voice, markedly in contrast with the thick tones of the Obersturmfuehrer.

Voss was tall and weedy and young; even in their thick gloves one could suspect the slim elegance of his hands. His uniform was natty and smart, and despite the prevailing conditions his boots maintained a high degree of polish. Yet for all his well-dressed appearance Voss gave an impression of wearing someone else's clothes.

He was clearly not a man born to wear uniform, and certainly not that black uniform with all its hated significance. At the moment he was deadly pale; the horrible things that had just been done on the terrace of the beerhouse made him feel faint and sick, but he was doing his best to conceal it, for it was not wise to allow himself any display of faintheartedness under the gaze of Obersturmfuehrer Engel—far more than being not wise it was hideously dangerous.

Voss had not yet become accustomed to horrors, despite the fact that the war was now far into its sixth year. He had believed the massive air raids on Berlin to be the climax of war's horrors until a month or more ago; and he had never witnessed the actual progress of one of those raids, always being safely in a bunker while they were going on. Until the late summer of 1945, in fact, he had led a sheltered life. His mother was a famous actress—one of the true Nordic type, thank God—and even though there was a certain mystery about who his father was, family influence, obscurely exerted, had kept him in safe places all through his adolescence and young manhood, able until he was twenty to move about in, and enjoy, the feverish society life of the capital, doing nothing in particular but with a handsome uniform to shelter him from inquiring glances. It was not until the appalling events that followed the attempt on Hitler's life—and the simultaneous military disasters in East and West—that he had been disturbed; then with Himmler and Goebbels in charge of total mobilization, fate had reached out for him at last. Family influence helped him even then for a time, succeeding in getting him appointed to the SS officers' school in Zehlendorf where he could normally expect six months' training without risk of his life. It had meant deplorably hard work, of course, and the Second Class Order of Civilian Service that he wore on his breast did not help to miti-ing into France, and the Russians came flooding over gate that, but rather the reverse.

But when the British and the Americans came burst-the frontiers of the Reich, the six months' training was cut short, and he had been hurried with thousands of others out to active service; and here he was, under the tutelage of Obersturmfuehrer Engel, seeing sights and performing duties which he would not have thought possible. Even so it might have been worse; if, on his arrival at Insterburg as a bewildered young subaltern, he had not found all communications in chaos he would have been sent into a fighting unit, and he might be dead by now. As it was he had been thrust into the SS police unit on the lines of communication, still momentarily safe. He was safe as long as the frail German line ten miles away continued to hold back the Russian forces, but when that line should break everything would be finished. Probably he would be shot, and in any case the best he could hope for would be a prison camp, starvation, cold, misery, forced labor, and young Voss feared them almost as he feared death.

Now here was something strange happening. A motor convoy was coming slowly up the road towards the dockyard gate. There were two uniformed motorcyclists in the lead and three large black cars following, and last of all a small truck piled high with baggage. Sirens and motor horns cleared the way along the road of the refugees who had crowded onto its surface. Up to the gate the convoy drove, and when they stopped, a smart officer—far smarter than Voss—climbed out of the leading car and walked up to the gate to address the sentries there. At the same time the refugees came swarming up, crowding round the cars, and as knowledge of the new development spread more and more people came surging towards the gate, far beyond the power of the two uniformed motorcyclists, now dismounted, to hold them back. A window in the leading car was lowered and a bulky man craned his head out of it. He gesticulated towards Engel's party.

"Herr Obersturmfuehrer! Keep these people back! Attend to your duty at once!"

"Gauleiter," muttered Engel out of the corner of his mouth to Voss. "Come on."

So that was the Gauleiter, the local embodiment of the Fuehrer's unlimited powers, the untrammeled overlord—until the arrival of the Russians—of two million people. His greatcoat concealed the orders that must cover his chest, but cap and greatcoat and gloves were in themselves sufficient indication of his greatness. There were other uniforms visible inside the cars and women as well, in smart hats and fur coats.

Engel, with Voss and the SS men beside him, flung himself at the mob pressing silently round the cars, beating them back; it was strange that the helpless miserable people uttered no sound at all, shrinking back before the blows dealt at them without a word or a cry, as if all this was something happening in a bad dream. The iron gate was rattling as it slowly opened; the officer who had got out climbed back into the car and slammed the door, and the three cars moved slowly forward into the dockyard. Voss caught a glimpse of the face of an elderly woman in the second car, as she looked out of the window. It was set in frozen horror, and Voss, glancing back over his shoulder, followed her gaze. The two corpses hanging from the beams in front of the beer-house were swaying in the wind, and as they turned slowly back and forward, to left and to right, they al-

ternately revealed and concealed the notices that dangled on their chests.

The gate clanged shut again, the bolts rattled, and
Engel and Voss were free to allow the mob to press up
towards that gate again, to stare through the bars between the sentries at the unattainable possibilities of
safety that lay beyond them. The funnels of steamships
were visible over the sheds and warehouses, mostly big
passenger ships; ancient ships that had been used for
years as floating barracks to house the submarine crews
in training, but nobody doubted that they could still
steam and steer, and nobody doubted that they would be
used to transfer the naval personnel from this base to
other ports along the Baltic shore, to Stettin or Lubeck
or Flensburg or over to Copenhagen, hundreds of miles
beyond the reach of the Russian armies mad with the
lust for blood. In those distant towns was safety. There
was shelter there, and food, and warmth, but above all
there was safety. Safety lay beyond the bars of that lofty
gate; on this side there was the certainty of torture, rape,
and murder.

The rasp of a key in a lock attracted the attention of
Engel and Voss, and they turned to see a side door in
the barrier open to reveal a naval officer issuing out
from the yard. The heavy coat in which he was muffled
bore no badges of rank, but the rim of gold round the
peak of his cap told them that he was a commander at
least. At sight of him the crowd began to swarm towards him, clutching at him, trying to attract his attention; the urgency of those panic-stricken people might
well have been fatal to him, they might have pulled him
down and trampled on him, if the SS men had not come

to his rescue, beating back the crowds and clearing a space round him in which he could speak to Engel comparatively undisturbed. Despite this experience he addressed Engel with an air of cool detachment, a conscious superiority based on something besides difference in rank; the navy, and more particularly the submarine branch of that service, felt themselves to be of a higher order of humanity than the SS, if indeed they admitted the claim of the SS to be humans at all. Voss admired the attitude, for he had not been properly indoctrinated, thanks to his faulty upbringing. The fact that the naval officer returned Engel's salute with an ordinary naval salute, despite the fact that for six months now the Hitler salute had been made compulsory among all ranks and services, might be attributed to absent-mindedness or long habit.

"The ships are about to leave," said the naval officer. "And there is an order from Fuehrer Headquarters to transport as many of these people as possible."

"How many, sir?" asked Engel.

The naval officer looked round him, at the enormous crowd packed as far as the eye could reach. He made his face an expressionless mask to conceal his astonishment, his bewilderment, and his dismay. He had heard that there were refugees clamoring at the dockyard gate, and in his mind's eye he had visualized some hundreds, even some thousands. Until now he had no idea that there were refugees by the hundred thousand awaiting transport. He was revising his estimates. The old *Kolberg*, for instance, was already comfortably filled with naval ratings and the invaluable dockyard personnel without whom the U-boat campaign could not well be carried on. He had thought that a couple of hundred refugees might perhaps be carried as well. Now his next thought was that some kind of accommodation might be found for five hundred. Then immediately he discarded the idea as utterly inadequate. There could be no question of accommodation. It was a matter of packing the ship full, for Copenhagen was little more than two hundred miles away, and the old *Kolberg* might still do twelve knots if her boilers lasted. Less than a day's run; there was no real reason against jamming her as tight with people as a Berlin bus in the rush hour. There would be no drinking water or food—it would be impossible to issue any even if there were enough—but the people would live through that short time without any. There was the question of stability, all the same; these herds of people on the upper decks of the *Kolberg*, uncontrolled and uncontrollable, might rush in panic to one side or the other, and this wind had whipped the Baltic into a raging hell. Ten people, fifteen people—might weigh a ton. How many tons of humanity could the *Kolberg* carry without endangering her stability? The naval officer allowed his mind to dwell for a moment on the theoretical problems of naval construction that had been set him in the old days at the marine academy, and then he forced himself to be rational. There could be no numbering of these people in any case. The *Kolberg* might take three thousand; the *Mittelmeer* as many; the smaller naval craft a few hundred each. He knew that the *Lorenzo* was already casting off and putting to sea with the Gauleiter on board—she was an old Hamburg-America liner and might have carried twenty thousand people. There was no chance of carrying even a tenth of these masses of people. Perhaps—if the army held out over there—there might be a return passage made, possibly two or three. For the present, however, it was necessary to make an estimate of some sort.

"A few thousand," said the naval officer, and then, desperately, "Say eight thousand."

That was an extreme maximum.

"Eight thousand, sir?" echoed Engel with a glance over the enormous marshaling yard. "We have fifty thousand here at least. More. And a quarter of a million in the city."

"Yes," said the naval officer, unhelpfully on account of the despair in his heart, and then he said something that might be considered more unhelpful still. "Once I open those gates—"

"It will be hard to hold this mob," said Engel, finishing the sentence.

"You will have to manage them in any case," said the naval officer. "There's no time to lose. And I told you the order came direct from the Fuehrer Headquarters."

"I'll control them, sir," said Engel.

Already they were walled in by a vast crowd of people whose eyes were watching their smallest movements.

"Let them move slowly in," said the naval officer. "I'll go back and make arrangements for gangways at the ships. I'll tell my petty officer to open the gates in five minutes."

"Five minutes, sir," said Engel, looking at his watch.

"And when I send you word that the ships are full—" said the naval officer.

"I'll shut the gates, sir."

The naval officer delayed to make a further suggestion.

"Women and children only?" he said, tentatively. There were many old men in the crowd.

"I'll try, sir," said Engel.

It was like fighting a rear-guard action to let the naval officer back through the side door. The mob had to be beaten back before the door could be quickly opened and shut again. A despairing cry went up from those people who saw the door shut, and, with no immediate action visible after the naval officer's departure, the cry was repeated and magnified as hysterical women began to scream questions and appeals to Engel. He had to shout to make himself heard by Voss.

"I'll only open half the gate," he bellowed. "I'll try to let 'em through a hundred at a time. Stand by the gate to shut it after each hundred, and only open it when I give the word."

"Very well," replied Voss at the top of his voice. It was incredible that here in the open air he had to shout because of the screaming of women, and yet it was true.

The platoon plowed its way through the mob again—only by the wildest efforts could the men move against that pressure—and took up its position in front of and to each side of the gate.

"Time's up," said Engel, and nodded through the bars to the naval petty officer of the guard. "Get back, there! Get back, there! No men, women and children only. No men!"

The petty officer drew the bolts of the gate and slowly opened one half of it, and with that there was an immediate and utter convulsion. The enormous power of a huge crowd of people intent upon a single object and hysterical beyond all control was manifest at once. The cordon of SS men ruptured. Voss, standing immediately in front of the opening, was swept backwards like a feather; he had the utmost difficulty in keeping his footing as he ran backwards before he could turn round and run with the mob; in that terror-stricken moment, when he nearly fell, he imagined himself beneath the feet of that torrent of humanity. If he had fallen he would have been trampled into a bloody jelly in no time. As it was he was swept back at the head of the advancing column, utterly helpless for fifty yards. At this point the speed of the rush died away by reason of the fanning out of the column, and Voss was able to disengage himself and run to the side. Dazed, he made his way back toward the gate, with the mob speeding in the opposite direction; humanity being forced through the gate with the irresistible violence of water from a fire hose. A single SS man showed up beside him; Engel and all the rest had been broken into two groups outside the barrier, far from the gate. Voss thought he heard a shot or two through the din, but he knew even in his bewildered mind that shooting would not stop this mob. Engel and the SS had much experience in the repression of masses, but no experience like this before.

At the gate the scene was frightful. Voss stood beside the unopened half, in the angle between the gate and the inrushing mass, as if he were in a quiet eddy of a raging river. At the threshold of the open gate the people entering were stumbling and then climbing upwards and then stumbling down; already there was a mound

of bodies there over which the mob was pouring. At his
very feet was a woman's hand, at the end of an out-
stretched arm—the rest of the woman was at the base of
that mound under the trampling feet. Against the bars
of the unopened half of the gate there were women and
old men pressed with flattening violence by the force behind. Voss could see two or three faces distorted in agony
although in the din he could not distinguish the individual screams that were issuing from the open mouths. Just
as there was an arm lying at his feet, so there was an arm
waving in his face, an arm thrust through the bars,
jerking convulsively—whose, he could not tell.

Beside him stood three or four of the naval guard,
quite bewildered. They were fingering their submachine
guns, but they had not opened fire. To spray machine-
gun bullets through those bars would only kill people
whose still-standing corpses would screen the rest of the
mob. There was only one thought in Voss's mind; he
must ease that awful pressure.

"Open the gate!" he said.

No one heard him; perhaps he had only addressed the
sentence to himself, for he moved forward to draw the
bolts. By hanging all his weight on it he was able to pull
down the upper one; before he could do anything about
the lower one it bent with the pressure upon it—thick,
heavy bar of iron though it was—and the gate swung in-
wards pushing him back before it, with the bent end of
the bolt plowing over the cobbles. Now although the entrance was doubled in width it did nothing to diminish
the pressure; it only meant that twice the number of
people were pouring in—at the newly opened half there
was instantly formed another mound of bodies over

which the mob came stumbling and climbing, carried by the rush behind. But at least the noise diminished noticeably, if only temporarily. Voss, standing appalled by the gate, heard a new sound now—the sound of shots from behind him, one or two at first and then the vicious chatter of a machine gun, repeated in a succession of bursts. That must be down by the ships; they must be firing there to keep back the mob storming on board.

The sound ended all the little that was left of Voss's self-control. Now he was nothing but a puppet pulled by the strings of unmitigated panic. There was no reasoning left in him; it was replaced by the logical unreason of the panic-stricken that swept him away towards the shooting. There was an uncontrollable sea of humanity before him; behind him was something that people were willing to fight for, to imperil their bodies for; panic turned him about to run for that precious thing, that faint yet yearned-for chance of escape. He ran like a madman, in his boots and heavy greatcoat. He ran like a madman, for indeed he was mad, insane temporarily at least. His breath issued from his throat in high-pitched hysterical sobs.

The incoming press of people entering through the gate spread much more thinly within the dockyard. Like torrents in gutters there were streams of people pouring down the passages between the sheds, stumbling and leaping over the railway tracks, winding about among the deserted trucks that stood on the rails; here a woman or a man might trip or fall and actually have a chance to rise again without being trampled to death. Voss dashed among them, thrusting people aside, breaking through hurrying groups; his body was young and fit and

stronger than these others, all strengthened equally by
panic. His eye caught the gleam of dark water in a dock
basin, and he swerved. He ran and he ran, still uttering
his high-pitched sobs. Here there was a vast crowd
packed against the water's edge, and beyond the crowd
the upper works of a ship, but no possibility of boarding
her with that crowd there. He swerved again, still running like a mad dog; more than once he crashed into
people hurrying in other directions and sent them flying.
He was skirting the dark expanse of water; once he had
to leap into the air to clear a couple of corpses that lay
together in a pool of blood and he had to twist and turn
to avoid masses of abandoned material that lay all along
the water's edge, cases and boxes of all descriptions. And
then he saw something else. On the far side of the basin
a little vessel—a tug—was drawing away from the bank.
She was leaving a screaming mob of people at the
water's edge, and she was turning around, backing across
the basin to do so, churning up the dirty dark water
under her low stern. Voss ran on as madly as ever towards her. The wailing of the crowd across the water
was blown to thin piercing shreds by the wind through
which Voss heard the sharp "ping" of the tug's engine-
room bell. The churning under her stern stopped, but
still she continued to drift backwards, silently and slowly
approaching Voss's side of the basin with her stern.
Another ping of the bell, and the churning under her
stern began again and her backward motion diminished.
It was the moment when she would be nearest to Voss,
and in that moment Voss sprang, in a leap he could
never have made if he had been in an ordinary mental
state. He soared through the air, and his feet just reached

the extreme edge of her low after-gunwale. There was no rail there—the vessel was a harbor tug—and with a convulsive wrench of his body he managed to fall forward, instead of backward into the water. The deck was crammed with people into whom he crashed. One foot slipped backwards over the edge again, but he recovered himself, twining his arms round the two women against whom he had fallen and sinking to his knees.

He knelt there for some seconds, his face nuzzling against the women's skirts, at the very limit of his physical powers. He grew slowly conscious of the rough material against which his face was pressed, and conscious of the jarring beat of the propeller under his knees. He was about to rise to his feet, his strength having returned, and then his full consciousness came back to him and he decided not to do so until he had composed himself. He was safe here in a ship, heading out to sea, and yet—he felt a cold chill pass down his sweating back as the realization came to him—he was not in the least safe. He had deserted his post of duty. He had run away. He was wearing a uniform that exposed him to the hatred of the masses as well as inspiring them with fear. A single question from the military police and he would be lost. He remembered the fate of the man with his arm concealed under his coat. Voss had to be ready with a glib answer the moment a question should be addressed to him. He had to be ready for anything.

Hysteria had vanished now, although terror remained, and terror goaded his imagination as he knelt. He had had much experience already, in Berlin cafés, of side stepping awkward questions about his duties, and it had made him nimble-witted; since that time he had passed briefly through the Zehlendorf officers' school and had had three weeks of active duty; he knew a good deal about the structure in which he had to find a fictitious niche. There occurred to him the sentence that Engel had frequently quoted to him, first enunciated by a Standartenfuehrer whom he admired: "Only hang one in ten. That's enough to make the others fight." The memory made him shudder again. But ideas were forming in his mind. The uniform he wore was dreaded as well as hated; although no one in the other branches of the armed services would lift a finger to help the SS if there were the barest excuse not to do so, on the other hand the SS could hold itself aloof and claim the independence resulting from orders from the highest sources. Voss stood up ready, or as nearly as he would ever be, for the next step.

Yet he was encompassed about by physical difficulties at the moment. His place on board the tug was precarious; as he stood there on the farthest aftermost inches of the tug's deck and with the low gunwale behind his knees he pressed himself against the solid mass of people in front of him. To retain his balance at all he had to clutch the two women against whom he had crashed when he made his jump; he made sure of his grip of them. There was no guessing at their social status from the bundled clothes they wore, with hoods over their heads, but one had a wrinkled face with a nose that bore the mark of spectacles now missing, and was probably elderly; the other might be in her forties and was no beauty. One thing was apparent; Voss's nose was close to them and was filled with the smell of sweating and unwashed humanity, acrid and distasteful. Nevertheless, that was nothing to cause surprise; the most elegant and pampered beauty from the Reichsmarschall's marble salons at Karinhall would smell like that if she had fled across the fields for days before the Russians without taking off her clothes. The two women stood like statues in his embrace, doing nothing either to break it or to ease his situation, and he ignored them after his first glance as he tried to put his plan into operation.

But there was nothing he could do at the moment, poised dangerously on the edge of the deck, which was slightly cambered here, turtle-backed, making his foothold more precarious than ever, and making it difficult to see over the heads of the crowd in front of him unless he stood on tiptoe, craning his neck. The tug was thumping her way ponderously across the bay, heading for the open sea. Behind them the city began to reveal itself despite its veil of smoke; already the wind blew with more piercing shrillness; already the tug was beginning to lift a little to small waves; already a splash or two of icy spray was coming up from under the counter; already there were wails of dismay from the packed people on the deck. Forward on the little bridge someone was bellowing orders. Stretching his neck to look at him, Voss could see him well enough even though the wind rendered his words unintelligible. The cap and uniform were unmistakable; he was a naval warrant officer, a boatswain or something of that sort, and Voss sighed with relief. If the captain of the tug were a mere boatswain—and the fact that he was the captain was obvious from the way he was giving orders—the subsequent steps would be easier.

The orders he was giving were having some effect, and

all to the good. The tense crowding of the deck suddenly diminished; people were moving back, there was room to breathe. It seemed likely that the captain had opened up some space below decks in the tug for the mob to move down into. The women at whom Voss was clutching moved back out of his embrace, and he was able to take a step forward away from the perilous edge of the deck. And now a couple of sailors were working their way along the fringe of the crowd; they carried coils of rope which they were stringing from stanchions, rigging lifelines which might keep the people from falling overboard—or from being washed overboard.

"Is that the captain up there?" asked Voss of one of the sailors. He had to repeat his question sharply to get a reply, for everyone within reach was asking questions and the sailor was concentrating on his work to avoid any necessity to answer the refugees.

"Yes," said the sailor at length.

Voss started to elbow his way through the now much more thinly packed crowd on the deck. He was trembling a little as he did so, not with cold but with anxiety. He had to try and master himself. The people against whom he pushed turned in angry resentment, and the first step towards self-mastery that he took was to snarl back at them with all the arrogance that might be expected of an SS officer, one carrying out an important duty. He pushed on through towards the bridge; in the lee abaft of it people were packed more thickly again, huddled together.

"Out of the way, you," growled Voss.

Reaching up he grasped a rail, and pulled himself up; the rails here, round the wing of the bridge, were closed in by a canvas dodger which concealed him until he had a foothold on the deck of the bridge and was beginning to swing himself over. The captain saw him out of the tail of his eye and swung round with his hand to his pistol holster, and two other men hurried up with iron bars in their hands; clearly they had already beaten back attempts to swarm onto the bridge. Voss forced himself to ignore the menace, forced himself to act in accordance with his certain knowledge that no one would raise a hand against the uniform that he wore. He stepped down onto the bridge in a pose of complete self-confidence; it was thanks to his actress mother, perhaps, that he was able to assume that attitude. And there had been one or two occasions in the past when he had faced the necessity of impressing headwaiters, so that they would give him credit; those experiences helped him now, too, with his life at stake.

"Heil Hitler," he said, with the stiffest and most rigid salute he could produce.

"Heil, Hitler!" was the reply with an abstracted half-lift of the arm.

"The captain of this tug?" he demanded loftily.

"Yes," said the warrant officer, and then he grudgingly added, "Sir."

The word told Voss that he had won the opening round of his battle against destiny.

"I am the bearer of important dispatches for the Gauleiter," he said.

"The Gauleiter?" repeated the tugmaster, his glance traversing round forward to where, already out at sea, the funnels of a ship and a smudge of smoke were still visible. "He sailed in the *Lorenzo*."

Voss had been quite sure that the Gauleiter would not have delayed in getting away to sea with his family.

"I am aware of that," he said, "I have to follow him and deliver these dispatches."

He allowed his hand as if unconsciously to tap his breast pocket.

"I understand," said the tugmaster, even though there was an undertone of doubt in what he said. He was an elderly weather-beaten man whose faded blue eyes were still hard and piercing. The tugmaster let those eyes travel slowly up and down this young man, obviously in his earliest twenties, but there was the uniform, there was the assured manner. Sons and nephews and cousins of important men often moved in the highest circles. In any case, as the tugmaster told himself, there was no useful action he could take. He could not turn back and put this young man on shore again. It would be unsafe to demand further credentials; no one willingly incurred the resentment of the SS. In Copenhagen the authorities would deal with the man if he were a deserter. Until then it would be best to leave well alone.

The tugmaster combined a kindly heart with a stern sense of duty. He had been ordered to destroy his tug, for the naval authorities had doubted if she could manage the long passage to Copenhagen in the prevailing weather conditions, and he had pleaded to be allowed to make the attempt, in full confidence that he would succeed. In that confidence he had also decided that perhaps he might take a dozen refugees with him; there would be sufficient accommodation for that number. He had been taken by surprise by the uncontrollable state of the mob, just as Obersturmfuehrer Engel had been.

When the rush came pouring on board he had been quite unable to deal with it; only by slipping the warps and steaming away from the edge of the basin had he succeeded in getting away at all, and then it had been with practically every inch of deck space occupied. Luckily the hatchways had been closed and no one had found his way down below. By opening the hatchways and cramming seventy people down below he had contrived to make breathing space for the remaining two hundred. He looked up at the gray sky, darkening now with the approach of evening; he heard the scream of the wind in the funnel stays; he felt the lift of the tug beneath his feet, and he shook his head in sick despair. He could not imagine—at least he could imagine too well—what would happen to his two hundred deck passengers during the coming night, with waves breaking over the low deck and freezing as they broke. Yet it was impossible to go back, and if he did, then nothing short of actual shooting—and possibly not even that—would drive those fear-crazed people off his deck back again into the inhospitable shore, while shooting would hardly keep the fear-crazed mob on shore from pouring on board. He looked down at his crammed decks, and bellowed further orders to his men for further lifelines to be rigged here, there, and everywhere, crisscross about the deck. They might do something to save those people, and canvas dodgers rigged where possible might keep out the worst of the sea.

Voss made himself lounge against the bridge rail in an attitude of elegant unconcern. It was only with the utmost effort of will that he kept his limbs from trembling and his teeth from chattering. Cold and fatigue were at work on him as well as fear and the reaction from his panic. The wind, even with the protection of the dodger, blew through him like a knife. He yearned frantically for rest and shelter, for an opportunity to relax. To make that opportunity for himself he must keep himself under control for some minutes longer. He straightened himself up from the rail; the small motion which the tug was displaying already disconcerted him, and so did the passive resistance of his weary legs, but he drove himself to maintain his appearance of unconcern. Three halting steps took him to the entrance into the tiny wheelhouse, and he glanced in. Two men there occupied nearly all the available space, but only nearly all.

He planned in his mind the best way to address the tugmaster. There must be the deference accorded by sea tradition to the captain of any vessel at sea, but it must be mingled with condescension of an SS officer towards a mere warrant officer of the navy, and yet a friendly condescension, implying that the deference was only a polite form. He must make it clear that he expected his suggestion to be accepted, and yet without so much of an air of taking things for granted as to rouse antagonism. And at that moment Voss realized with shocking clarity that he was just a coward, running away from danger, and he must not allow that to affect his attitude. He must remember, he must keep it firmly in the forefront of his mind, that he was an officer of unsullied honor, and consequently of clear conscience, engaged upon vitally important duty for Fuehrer, Reich, and people.

"I shall rest, I think, Captain," he said. "I think there is room in here for me."

Without waiting for an answer he lounged slowly into the wheelhouse; the thick steamy warmth inside was marvelously comfortable. The man at the wheel and the man at the voice tube and telegraph—some sort of petty officer, this—did not spare him a glance. He squeezed himself into the corner; and lowered himself down to the deck, sitting in the angle of the bulkhead aft. He let his head droop—wonderful that he no longer had to keep his chin up—and his head drooped farther and farther; he rested his arms on his knees and his face on his arms. This was what he wanted; there was a black whirlpool of thought slowly circling in the inner recesses of his mind, but the fog of fatigue obscured it. He was a coward—a coward—he had joked about it to himself all these years, but with the hope that when the time came he might prove braver than he thought, and the failure of the hope was painful despite his cynical realism. And tomorrow in Copenhagen he would have to think fast and act quickly so that he would not be detected as a deserter, as a coward—he was a coward—the whirlpool completed its circle, but he was so drained of strength that even so he slept, with his face on his arms.

It was not for long that he slept; his frightful fatigue could only keep him unconscious for a short length of time in the conditions that were developing round him. He awoke in complete confusion, in an insane darkness, a darkness that was filled with dreadful noises, a darkness that leaped about, that struck him from the sides and that heaved him up from underneath, that fell away beside him unexplainedly and seemingly interminably. It took more than a few moments for him to understand what was happening. The wheelhouse canted far over so that he slid on the deck and brought up sharply against the bulkhead; the next slide carried him against a pair of human legs and somebody kicked him violently and a voice growled "Keep clear." He struggled backwards into a sitting position, and with his hands spread on the deck on either side of him, he was able to hold himself there against the next upheaval. With each heave of the tug there came the noise of wild battering, like massive hammers, but there were a myriad other voices too. Through the deck beneath him came the sound of human voices wailing; the wailing rose and fell as did the tug, and although it attracted his attention first by reason of its intermittent pitch it was by no means the loudest noise; the loudest noise was the screaming of the wind, high and almost unfluctuating, and there was other screaming as well, not so audible, and thumpings and bangings.

Now he was going to be sick. He managed to check himself for the moment, surprised though he was by his nausea. The tug must undoubtedly be sinking. He would be drowned here in the little wheelhouse. He got to his knees and grasped for the handle of the door and opened it by a miracle. As he turned it, another roll of the tug hurled him forward out through the opening door. He fell into other people here on the wing of the bridge; his hands felt the slippery surface of wet oilskins.

"Who are you?" demanded a loud voice.

"The SS officer," said Voss.

The tug heeled over again in the darkness, unbelievably far, and flung him back again against the wheelhouse. The wind tore at him, and a great mass of icy salt water flung itself against his face and chest with stunning force. Voss found his hands on the rail and was able to hold on, and then he vomited dreadfully into the wind; for some seconds he had no other thought. The wind shrieked again and the tug rolled and pitched, heeling in every direction in rapid succession. Voss was almost blinded with spray and in the black night his watering eyes could see almost nothing; he was looking aft (although he did not know it) into the wind and all he could see was the faint white gleam of breaking waves. But below him, from the huddled crowd on the afterdeck, he heard, as the tug went over again, a horrible wild cry, "A—a—ah," even through the wind. The weight of his body wrenched at his shoulder joints as he clutched the rail, and the deck canted under his feet.

He knew that the wheelhouse door was close beside him. He fumbled for it and found the handle again, opened it and fell in, helpless on the deck while the door shut with a shattering crash behind him. Now he almost did not care if the tug sank or not. Somebody trod on him, somebody kicked him, somebody dragged him into the corner he had previously left. There his hand found a pipe that it could clutch, and it hung onto it without his conscious volition, preventing him from sliding as he lay on the deck, helpless with seasickness and fear. Outside, on the sea-swept decks, the women and children and old men were slowly dying of exposure.

Not long after he re-entered the wheelhouse there was sudden new action, gruff orders given and curt replies. Voss was vaguely conscious of a different behavior on the part of the tug, of some seconds when her balance

seemed even more precarious than it had ever been, of
a seemingly more uncontrolled movement, and then a
steadier, more purposeful movement of the tug, up and
down, pitching forward and aft, with a slighter roll, and
yet with the crashing of the waves more intensified. Cold
air suddenly filled the wheelhouse, and great quantities
of icy water. It surged, some inches deep, back and forward over the deck in the wheelhouse; as it drained
away through the opened door it was continually re-
supplied by the water which came tumbling in through
the opened windows of the wheelhouse. It was impossible
to lie on the deck; Voss found the hinged seat and sat
himself on it with the water splashing round his ankles.
He could still hold onto the pipe with rigid hands and
he writhed now and then in paroxysms of seasickness.

He knew nothing about all the wild work that had
been going on, nor of all the desperate things that had
been done on the sea-swept deck. The captain had decided to heave-to; he had swung the tug round, bows
onto wind and sea, and he had contrived to pay out a
hundred feet of towing hawser from the bow, which,
dragging out as the tug went off to leeward, acted as a
sea anchor to keep her in position. But there had been
fifty people crammed on the tiny foredeck, already stiff
and cold and dying from their two hours' exposure.
They had had to be forced or dragged away, and terrible choices had to be made. There was not shelter
below decks in the tug for one tenth of the refugees. The
stronger and more able-bodied of those below had to be
forced out to make room for the perishing—forced out
into the bitter cold of the afterdeck, although now with
the tug hove-to, the bridge afforded some sort of lee for

a good deal of that deck. There they had to be bound into position like bundles of firewood and left in the storm.

Riding to her sea anchor, the tug faced the short steep waves of the Baltic. Many of those waves burst over her foredeck; that was why the windows of the wheelhouse had been lowered, as otherwise they would be driven in, and the flying glass would be more dangerous than any water. There was danger that the whole superstructure might be carried away, in which case the gaping remnants of the hull would fill and sink in a few seconds; there was danger that under the strain of the constant working and pounding the wretched hull might open up like a basket. But, on the other hand, despite the resistance of the dragging hawser, the tug was steadily going to leeward—to the westward, to possible safety —at a very respectable rate, perhaps as much as four miles an hour. The engines could be throttled down and precious fuel saved, although they still had to be continuously employed driving the pump that cast out the water which found its way into the straining hull above and below.

To the tugmaster, working with his men through that awful night, it seemed unbelievable that he should have attempted to weather a winter gale in his sixty-foot harbor tug. But it was far more unbelievable that he should have had to do the other things; that he should have had to hound wailing women from out of the warmth and shelter of below deck up into the killing cold. It was unbelievable that the Russians should be in Konigsberg, that the Reich should be falling in ruins, that the advent of the Nazi Party should have resulted in all these horrors, that in the comparative shelter of his wheelhouse should be a young able-bodied man while women and children died of exposure on his open deck; unbelievable but true; it was all part of the same picture.

Like a half-submerged bit of wreckage the harbor tug *Tell IV* went drifting across the Baltic in the darkness of that January night; it seemed as if the waves must in the end overwhelm her as they burst over her, but each time she wallowed free, sluggishly, out of the foaming smother; hour after hour she drifted, with the engineers toiling feverishly to keep her pump from choking, and while the women and old men and children died one by one out on the afterdeck. The captain and his men found the stiff corpses by touch as they worked their way round the deck through the long northern night. And in that packed mass of humanity there was shelter to be found in the center, in the lee afforded by the bridge. And the frantic people, numbed and yet still conscious of the freezing wind and driving spray, sought always to work their way into the center of the mass, so that in that center where they sought safety many found death as they fell beneath the surging feet; sheep die like that when they huddle together for shelter beside a wall.

By imperceptible degrees the winter night gave way to the winter day, inexpressibly gloomy and gray. In the wheelhouse Voss discovered that all was not dark, that he could actually see, as his wavering eyelids opened just enough to let in the faint light; he still sat in the corner of the wheelhouse half dead with cold and sea-sickness. He rose precariously to his feet, shivering violently. There was no one at the wheel—he was alone in the wheelhouse, and for a space he knew fear again, until he glanced out aft and could just see the people there. He looked forward and saw the racing whitecapped rollers hurrying towards the bows; he felt the tug leap frantically again, like a goaded horse, rising nearly vertically (so it seemed) to the wave, hang there for one half of a second, and then quickly reverse her slope, stern upwards, bows down with the white foam roaring over the deck and thundering against the bridge—another moment of terror before the tug's bows lifted once more to repeat the convulsion. Voss hung on, watching those waves in solitary fascinated horror.

Later in the morning, with a heavy tramp of feet on iron decks, the captain and his mate, booted and oil-skinned, came running up to the bridge and stood out on one of the wings pointing and staring, the wind blowing their clothes stiffly out while the captain tried to focus his binoculars on the surface of the sea despite the wild leaping of the tug. It took Voss some seconds to perceive what was interesting them, and then he saw. There was wreckage floating on the surface; something like a packing case came slowly along the side of the tug, from stern to bow, and then other fragments, revealed and concealed alternately by the lift of the waves as the wind drove the tug steadily stern first across what must be a wide patch of wreckage. Now there were dead men in sight, six of them. Four wore life jackets which held their heads and shoulders above the surface on occasions. They bobbed, and rose and fell, and sometimes gyrated slowly in what might well be called a dance of death. The other two wore inflated collars which only just held their heads above the surface at best, appearing and disappearing, the water covering their blind faces most of the time; three times those faces reappeared, not twenty yards from the tug, before they passed forward out of Voss's sight. The captain shook his head as he took his binoculars from his eyes; he knew too well of the crowded ships that had left harbor before *Tell IV*. Russian submarines had been lying in wait out there, and despite the darkness and storm they had succeeded in sending their torpedoes home. How many dead? Five thousand? Ten thousand? None would be saved of all the thousands that had crowded the decks of those big ships. It would be a disaster beside which the loss of the *Titanic* would be insignificant, an unbelievable catastrophe—there was that word "unbelievable" again.

And things that had been unbelievable during the night were still more unbelievable during the day, with daylight in which to observe them. There was the awful business of trying to maintain a system of shifts between the refugees who were out on deck and those in the suffocating warmth of below decks. The captain endeavored to conscientiously do this, and his crew, redeyed and weary, tried to help him. It was a horrible thing to do; the women down below, packed, literally, as close as sardines, resisted wildly, wailing and sobbing and clinging on when the men tried to force them out on deck. There was death out on deck; there were stiff frozen corpses to be dragged to the side and dropped over. One third of the people who had stood there yesterday were dead now; perhaps that was lucky, as it gave the others more chance to survive; they could all crowd under the lee of the bridge where there was some shelter from wind and spray. As the women had to be dragged

out from below, so those on deck had to be dragged into
the minute quarters of the crew, not because they were
unwilling, but because many of them were too stiff and
frozen to move; and all this time the *Tell IV* never
ceased her wild movements, rearing up before the waves,
plunging down over them, not once or twice, or three or
four times, or ten or twenty times, but thousands of
times. The people were cut and bruised; the ones against
the lifelines were lacerated by the ropes when the *Tell
IV,* rearing up, pressed them against the ropes with all
the weight of the rest of the people upon them, old bones
broke like sticks. It helped to reduce the crowd.

It was unbelievable that this should go on through
the day and through the next night, and yet it did. The
gale blew unabated for twenty-four hours, while the *Tell
IV* drifted stern first before it, no hand at her wheel,
with no turns from her propeller. Not until late afternoon did the gale moderate in the least, and even then
it still blew fiercely while veering southerly a little, but
nobody on board, not even the captain, dazed with
fatigue, was aware of it. There was thirst to combat too
as time went on. Hunger could wait but not thirst. Voss
was given a mug of warm water to drink during the afternoon. Actually until he held it in his hand he had not
realized that he was half mad with thirst, but he knew it
as soon as he held the mug to his lips, he knew it as he
poured the life-giving stuff down his throat. He held the
mug out and croaked a request for it to be refilled, a
prayer, but the stupid seaman who gave it to him shook
his head. There was no water to spare on board, even
with a dwindling passenger list.

It was during the second night, after midnight, that

the wind appreciably abated. The motion of the *Tell IV* ceased to be quite as frantic, and the wind, blowing from the south instead of from the southeast, was not quite as murderous in its cold. Voss shared the wheelhouse that night with members of the crew, who came in, two at a time, to sleep, snoring prodigiously, for two-hour stretches, jammed beside Voss against the bulkhead. Even the captain slept there, for one single hour, leaving for that period the labor of trying to keep the refugees alive to his mate. For in the dawn there was work to be done. The hawser to which they had ridden for so long had to be got in; with the propeller turning again the *Tell IV* had to be handled delicately in the trough of the waves with a good hand at the wheel; much of the power had to be devoted to the pump, which by now was only just sufficient to keep down the water which came pouring on board through the myriad strained seams of the battered tug. They could not guess where they were; no one could tell how far, or in which direction, the gale had drifted them. The captain could only set an easterly course, and the *Tell IV* plodded steadily along it, to the thumping of her propeller, rolling hideously in the cross-swell; the changed motion reawoke Voss's seasickness, utterly empty though he was. Thirsty, hungry, cold, and seasick, and inexpressibly weary, he thought nobody could possibly be as miserable as he was. On the after-deck people were still dying.

It was noon when the captain, staring ahead through his binoculars, uttered a hoarse cry, lowered the glasses to rest his eyes, and then peered forward again into the haze.

"A ship!" he said.

The words brought life to Voss, but it was some time before, peering forward, he could see the distant mast and funnels. He had hardly caught sight of it when a searchlight began to wink at them, dot-and-dashing in the Morse code across the white and gray water. The captain looked round him in despair. His searchlight had been carried away on the first night—it was a miracle that the whole bridge had not carried away—and how could he reply to the question "What ship's that?" He could only head steadily forward, trusting to the obvious innocence of his intentions. The searchlight winked and winked.

"Swedish destroyer," said the captain, recognizing the upper works of the ship. She was making no effort to approach, and the captain guessed the reason. The *Tell IV* was in the midst of a Swedish minefield, laid to protect Swedish neutrality—Swedish national existence—from the encroachments of Germans and Russians. Below the tug was hidden death, hundreds of tons of high explosive, and she was churning her way steadily over it, thanks to her shallow draught. Let but one of those mines have taken up a slightly less depth than average, or if the waves over which *Tell IV* was steaming should lower her down farther than usual, and she would be blown into fragments. The captain did not speak of his anxieties; he could only stand and wait as the tug headed forward. In the haze beyond the destroyer there was now a hint of land—safety, warmth, and an end of harrowing responsibility.

The Swedish destroyer had her guns trained on the tug; in the world as it was she was taking no chances, for enemies might come leaping over the horizon from any quarter—neutrals could only remain neutral by being ready to defend themselves. All the destroyer could see was a battered harbor tug limping through the mine-fields, but no one could be sure of anything. The most innocent appearance might conceal some new invention, might herald some new and devilish plan, something more cunning than the Trojan horse. As the tug came on, the destroyer maintained her distance from her, guns still trained. The land was much nearer now. The searchlight winked once more, a brief message.

"Stop," said the captain, and rang down to the engine room.

The steady thumping of the engine ceased; the tug swung her nose into the waves, and an occasional signal down to the engine room called for a kick or two from the propeller to hold her steady. Swooping up and down over the waves from the destroyer came a boat, tinier and even more fragile than the *Tell IV*. The boat circled the tug; Voss could see the oilskins of the life-jacketed crew, the faces of the men looking keenly at the new arrival. Now the boat was running alongside; there were wild moments of churning water, as the tug soared on a crest and the boat sank into a trough. And then a uni-formed officer leaped from boat to tug, landing on the afterdeck, his hand to his pistol butt the moment he steadied himself. He stood aghast at what he saw on the afterdeck, rigid, while the boat maneuvered back into position and a couple of seamen leaped to the deck be-side him. He came forward towards the bridge, swaying on the heaving deck, the seamen following him appalled at what they saw. It needed only a brief explanation in German between officer and captain, only a brief signal from the tug to the destroyer, only a brief reply—"Follow me."

Voss came lurching out from the wheelhouse towards the Swedish lieutenant. He jerked out his right hand.

"Heil Hitler."

It was a military salute, from an officer of the armed services of one nation to an officer of the armed services of another nation with which it was at peace. The lieutenant gave a glance at Voss's uniform and returned the salute curtly.

"Your pistol, please," was all he said, holding out his hand, and Voss handed the weapon over without demur.

At once the lieutenant turned to address the captain, ignoring Voss.

The gale still blew, the *Tell IV* was still soaring up and swooping down on the waves, but Voss had forgotten his seasickness. Just over there was Sweden, and he was in the hands of the Swedish government. No doubt whatever but he would be interned. It was unbelievable good fortune. There would be no need to explain himself to suspicious military police in Copenhagen, there was no chance of dangling from a rope, no chance of having to take his place in a trench to face the onslaught of charging Russian tanks. A jangling buoy went by on the starboard side; the tug was nearing a headland, and now they were rounding the tip of a breakwater; it was unbelievable, the transition from rough to smooth water, the sudden steadiness of the tug, the orderly thumping of the engines, the moderation of the wind. The tug was turning to lie alongside a pier. A blue-and-gold flag was blowing out stiffly in the breeze, and a small guard of soldiers was forming up there, and Voss's eye was quick to note the subtle and indefinable difference between those soldiers and the last soldiers he had seen, men who had fought for their lives in the cause of a tottering empire.

On board the tug they were opening up the hatchway, and recoiling from the horrible stench which came pouring up, thick and warm, from down below. Two Red Cross ambulances, summoned presumably by wireless from the destroyer, were driving up to meet the tug when she should tie up; trim, neat ambulances, unmarked by war. Voss was terribly fatigued, he was wild with thirst, he was faint with hunger, but a line was being passed ashore and willing hands were looping it round a bollard. The war was over for him, and soon he would be unbelievably at peace, while twenty thousand corpses washed hither and thither in the stormy Baltic, while the Russian hordes poured into Germany, and while the world went down in ruin. But he had the feeling that even in a ruined world there would be a place for him.

THE HOSTAGE

It was in the autumn of 1944, when the Allied armies had come bursting out of the Cotentin Peninsula, flooding ácross France and advancing towards the frontiers of the Fatherland, that General of Infantry Friedrich von Dexter received his new orders. They were brought by motorcycle dispatch rider to the little house in the Welfenstrasse, having presumably been teletyped to Army District Headquarters from the Higher Command of the Armed Forces. Air raids on the town had been infrequent lately; and the ruins had ceased to smoke, but traffic was scanty, so that the roar of the motorcycle engine was heard by everyone, and neighbors peeped out of their windows to find out what was happening. They saw the General himself at his front door receive the envelope and sign the receipt for it, and then the motorcycle roared away again and the General went back inside his house.

Indoors the General found it hard to read the typewritten sheet with its printed heading, for the General was not wearing his spectacles and he had to hold the message at arms' length, which was inconvenient as the shattered windows had been boarded up, making the stuffy old-fashioned sitting room almost dark. Aloise, his wife, stood motionless by him while he read the message, motionless because as a soldier's wife she was trying to conceal the anxiety she felt. Dexter handed it to her without a word when he had finished reading it, and she read it with less difficulty.

"Does this mean—?" she began, and then she cut the question short. There were factory workers billeted in the house, and although they were presumably asleep, having been on the night shift, she could not risk being overheard discussing orders which had come from the Fuehrer himself. The two old people substituted glances for words; even in that twilit room they understood each other, after forty years of married life. The General looked over at the marble clock on the mantlepiece—the gift of the 91st Infantry on the occasion of their colonel's promotion—and reached a decision.

"We have ten minutes," he said. "Let us go for a walk."

They went out into the shattered streets; there, among the hurrying pedestrians, and the cyclists bumping their way over the uneven surfaces, they could talk safely as long as they did not display any deep emotion. The General was in civilian clothes, because when he had been dismissed from his command by a frantic Fuehrer-order he had been deprived of the right to wear uniform. So he wore his battered twenty-year-old tweeds, and Aloise walked beside him in her old-fashioned coat and skirt; and they appeared, as indeed they were, survivors of a past generation—even though, thanks to his spare figure and straight back, and with his hat concealing his white hair, the General's age was not apparent.

"What does it mean, dear?" asked Aloise before they reached the first corner.

"A direct order from the Fuehrer," said the General. "I have been appointed to the command of Fortress Montavril."

"Yes, dear. That is in France?"

"The Belgian frontier. Near the Channel Coast."

"What sort of fortress is it?"

The General looked casually round him, back over his shoulder, before he answered.

"I doubt if it is any fortress at all," he said. "I am quite sure there is none, in fact."

"But dear—?"

The General looked over his shoulder again.

"The Fuehrer has a new system," he said. "It began in Russia last year—no, two years ago. He designates a particular area as a 'fortress' and he appoints a garrison and a commandant for it."

"And then, dear? And then?"

"Because it has been designated a fortress the place is expected to hold out to the last man."

"I understand," said Aloise.

It was hard, dreadfully hard, to have to carry on this conversation in public, while trying to appear as if merely taking a casual stroll.

"There is much for you to understand, dear," said the General. "He is obsessed with this idea. And he still believes, in spite of everything, that what he wishes must come true. A place is a fortress and so it must hold out, no matter what the conditions. A barbed-wire perimeter —that is all that is necessary. Disorganized troops—

worn-out guns—shortage of ammunition—to speak of them is treason."

They could not exchange a significant glance here in the street; they must stroll along looking idly about them as if talking of nothing except trivialities.

"It is hopeless, then?"

"My duty—" began the General, and then he paused while making the effort to marshal all the multitudinous ideas called up by that word, the most significant in the vocabulary of a soldier. "It is my duty to obey my orders, and to fight for my country, no matter what the future."

"Of course, dear."

"But—" The General paused again, as a soldier well might pause after saying "but" when speaking of his duty.

"But what, dear?"

"That is not all. In a siege—"

The General had been married forty years. During that time he had come gradually to discuss professional matters with his wife in a way that often violated the convention that a wife should confine her interests to church, children and kitchen; but it was hard to convey to her in a few words the same picture of a siege that he carried in his mind's eye, called up with the ease of long professional experience.

"In a siege, dear?"

"There comes a time when further defense is useless. When the perimeter is broken. When the enemy has captured the commanding heights. When his artillery is overwhelming. Until then the garrison has been doing what it was intended to do. It has detained a larger force

in its front. It has caused more casualties than it has
suffered. Probably it has blocked some important line of
communication. But after that moment is reached—"

The General talked with the fluency he could display
when discussing professional subjects—he had talked in
this way to several generations of young men at the war
academy many years ago. He broke off now, for they
were passing a long line of people waiting outside a
shop. When they had passed it Aloise recalled him to his
explanation.

"You were talking about a siege, dear."

"Yes. So I was. After a certain point defense usually
becomes futile. The besiegers have an overwhelming artillery, good points of observation, have breached the
defenses. Then the losses become heavy among the de-
fenders with no corresponding loss to the besiegers. To
hold out longer than that means a massacre; men are
killed with no chance of hitting back. Sometimes it is
necessary, even so."

"It is hard to see why, dear." Aloise tried to speak
with a professional tone. Womanlike, her first reaction
when "casualties" were mentioned was not to think of
figures in a return, or of a commanding officer deciding
that a unit was "fought out," but of dead men and tortured men, of childless mothers and widowed wives—
of herself when the news came about their sons. She
knew that was not the way a General's wife should
think at a time when professional subjects were under
discussion, and she steadied her voice in consequence.

"It may happen," explained Dexter, "that the garrison
may still be blocking some important lane of communi-

cation. Then it may be worth while to incur those losses, to fight to the last man to keep that line blocked for the last few hours. It might be worth any sacrifice."

"I suppose so," agreed Aloise doubtfully.

"But that is an unusual situation," went on Dexter, "rarer than you would think."

Aloise in her heart of hearts, believed that there could never be any situation worth the sacrifice of thousands of lives, but she did not say so. She waited dutifully for her husband to continue.

"Generally speaking," he said, "a neutralized garrison under final attack has no useful part to play."

Aloise could make no contribution to the conversation, and her husband, interpreting her silence as lack of full understanding, went on to produce a specific instance, even though when lecturing to budding staff officers he had been careful to warn them not to think exclusively along arithmetical lines.

"Supposing," he said, "I have twenty thousand men in my garrison. That's a likely number. For two or three weeks I detain forty thousand of the enemy in front of me. Well and good. They attack at the decisive points. If their armor is not overwhelmingly strong I inflict heavy casualties on them. By the time they have mastered those decisive points I have lost—say five thousand men."

Aloise tried to picture five thousand dead men, and failed.

"But the enemy has lost ten thousand—twelve thousand, perhaps," went on her husband. "That is well and good, as I said. Now my guns are wearing out, my ammunition failing, and I am under constant searching bombardment. The assault is going to succeed whenever the enemy cares to make it. If I fight on, my fifteen thousand men are killed. And what does the enemy lose? One thousand? I doubt if it would be as many as that."

"I see," said Aloise, nodding her head as she walked.

The General looked at his watch. "My dear," he said. "I—I am afraid we must turn back."

Aloise glanced sharply at him, sidelong, at that break in his voice. It would have told her, even if she had not already guessed, how deep were his feelings, and how great was the strain he was enduring. After they had turned back he added a supplement to his little lecture.

"You might think," he said, "that it did not really matter. One garrison more or less— But that is not true. There is the rest of the army to think about. And there is the Germany of the future."

The General turned almost self-conscious as he entered into a discussion of the psychology of warfare. It was a very theoretical subject for a practical soldier.

"Soldiers will always fight under good officers. You can ask for extraordinary sacrifices from them." The General paused, and his faded blue eyes looked out over dreadful distant vistas of memory. "But they will not endure the thought of their lives being thrown away uselessly. They sulk, they desert. They shirk their duty. Once let it be known that they are going to certain death to no purpose and and—no garrison would ever hold out. Do you understand that, dear?"

"I understand," said Aloise.

"Already the army is not what it was."

The General looked quickly over his shoulder after he had said that. It had slipped out, and if he had been

overheard he might be a dead man that very night—
and die a shameful death at that. They walked on their
homeward way for some hundred yards in silence; the
General was silent not merely because he was shaken by
the risk he had just run but because he found it hard to
continue with what he had to say, to advance the conversation to the next stage. It may have been accidental,
or it may not, that Aloise made it easy by her next question.

"And you, dear?" she asked. "Have you thought
about what you will do?"

"I have my orders," said Dexter. There was a grim,
hard tone in his voice, and the glance that Aloise directed at him showed her that his face bore a bleak hopeless expression.

Most people would have thought there was very little
about General Friedrich von Dexter for any woman to
love, a professional soldier, hard, tough, limited both in
his education and outlook, and more than sixty years
old. Some men might laugh at him, some even despise
him, although there had been many young men who had
admired him, and there had been young captains who
had loved him, back in the days of that other nightmare,
when his fighting spirit alone had held his regiment
together in face of utter disaster at the Butte de Warlen-
court. And long after that, too; only last year at Khar-
kov, after he had fought his way with the remnants of
his army corps out of the ring of encirclement, his staff
had been moved to the deepest pity and sympathy when
the savage message arrived from headquarters depriving
him of his command. "The weak-kneed gentleman with
a von to his name" was how that message had described

him. Sorrow at losing him had been the first and principal emotion of those young staff officers. The feeling
that something must be desperately amiss at Fuehrer
Headquarters for such a message to be sent came only
secondarily—and of course could not be expressed in
any spoken words.

And the hard professional soldier had read that message without allowing his expression to change in the
least. He had left with only the briefest good-bys, to return home in disgrace, humiliated; only Aloise, when
she welcomed him home, knew the depths of that humiliation. And she loved him; perhaps she loved him the
more. An old woman of sixty, an old man of sixty-two,
walking together along the shattered street in the bleak
autumn sunshine, and discussing horrors, discussing the
death of twenty thousand men—how could there be love
there? Yet there was, just as flowers grow among the
rocks.

"I have to obey," said Dexter.

"I know you must, dear," said Aloise.

Even if there were no question of duty one obeyed
orders from the Fuehrer, or died.

"My dear," said Dexter, looking straight before him,
not daring even for a moment to meet his wife's eyes; it
was as if, although speaking low, he were addressing the
horizon.

"Yes, dear?"

"You know there is a Law of Hostages?"

"Yes."

"Do you understand about it?"

"Yes."

No one in Germany could fail to understand it. The

law had been promulgated that summer, although it had been in operation, to everyone's knowledge, long before. Now it had been announced in cold print. Men's families were to be held responsible for their actions. If a man were to desert, his father or his mother, his wife or his sister or his children would be killed. Not only the man who deserted, but the man who faltered in his duty, the man whose spirit failed him, the man who could not overcome his physical weaknesses, condemned in that moment those who were dearest to him to a death which might or might not be speedy. There was to be no human weakness displayed in the defense of the Third Reich and in the prolongation of the lives of the inhuman creatures who ruled it.

"You are the only one now, dear," said Dexter, still addressing the horizon.

"I know," said Aloise.

The younger Friedrich von Dexter had died at El Alamein; Lothar von Dexter at Stalingrad, Ernst was "missing, believed killed" at Rostov. There were only the two old people left. One would command at Montavril, and one would be a hostage at home.

"Did you notice in my orders who was to be my chief of staff?" asked Dexter.

"A Gruppenfuehrer—I can't remember his name at the moment, but I did not know it. An SS officer, of course?"

"Gruppenfuehrer Frey," said Dexter. "I don't know him either. But I know why he has been appointed."

"To spy on you?"

"To keep me up to my duty," said Dexter.

They were nearly home again now. Everything had

been said except good-by which would have to be said immediately.

There were several good-bys of the same sort being made at that time in Germany. Hitler was recalling to service many of the generals he had previously dismissed in disgrace, and appointing them to the command of "fortresses." He needed officers of high rank and authority, officers of experience, for those posts, to make sure the troops would obey. And he could rely on the Law of Hostages to make the generals themselves obey, however harshly he had treated them previously, and whatever their feelings towards him—about which he could have no doubt. As Dexter kissed his wife good-by before going out to the waiting car he had the Law of Hostages in his mind.

On the seventeenth day of the siege of Montavril the Allies launched their third attack, and succeeded in breaking through the outer perimeter of the defenses and in overrunning the whole of the area beyond the canal which the German forces had so far contrived to maintain. It was a desperate fight, in driving rain. The General himself had taken part in it. It was he personally who had saved the day. He had rallied the broken infantry, had brought up his last reserve, and had plugged the gap which yawned in the defenses between the canal and the crossroads. He himself had posted the guns, and by his own example had kept them firing. The counter-attack which he had launched might even have succeeded in regaining the vital higher ground beyond the crossroads if it had not been for the shell which momentarily disabled him. It had wounded his aide-de-camp, and had torn to pieces the brigadier a few yards from him, but by some freak of ballistics the fragment which struck the General on the shin did not even break a bone. But he had been dazed and shaken by the explosion and by the time he could stand steady on his feet again the counterattack had failed, and the battle had died away into desultory firing. The heavy rain limited visibility on all sides, turning the low fields into swamps, soaking— and perhaps in some instances even drowning—the helpless wounded who lay in the ill-defined no man's land round the crossroads. Perhaps the Allies would send in a flag of truce to arrange a brief armistice to attend to them.

The General left instructions on the matter with the colonel now in command of the sector before he went limping off—alone, because he left his runner to look after his aide-de-camp—to inspect the defenses along the canal bank. Here the Allies were already in touch, in a manner of speaking. With extraordinary celerity they had brought up a loud-speaker which was braying ceaselessly across the nearly dry canal bed. It spoke almost perfect German—the sort of German one might expect from a German-American who had used the language at home in his childhood—and it was appealing to the troops to give up a hopeless struggle. The General listened to it with the division commander at his side. Normally the penalty for listening to Allied broadcasts was death, the same as for possessing an Allied leaflet, but in these circumstances the penalty could hardly be exacted—too many of the garrison were within hearing. It was good sense that the loudspeaker talked, too, pointing out that now the Allies had direct obser-

vation over the whole of the defenses, and that there was
no part of the perimeter now which was not subject to
enfilade. The sensible thing to do would be to surrender,
said the loud-speaker, and if the mad folly of the officers
prevented that, then it would be equally sensible to desert, to slip over to the Allied lines where honorable
treatment awaited anyone who accepted the invitation.
The General listened, with the rain beating down on his
helmet and waterproof coat.

"I am going back to headquarters now," he said to the
division commander. "If they telephone for me, say that
I am on my way."

"Very well, sir," said the division commander.

He was a man in his forties, white with fatigue and
with red rims to his eyes. He watched with something
like envy the stiff figure of the man in his sixties, limping solitary down the muddy path; but there was pity
mingled with the envy.

The briefness of Dexter's journey from his outer defenses by the canal to his headquarters in the church of
Montavril demonstrated vividly the difficulties of the
defenses. It took Dexter not very long, even though he
had to pick his way. Here was a score of dead horses,
already beginning to bulge with corruption—there was
no fuel with which to burn them nor labor available to
bury them. The General thought bitterly of how the Allies, fully mechanized, had not a horse in their organization. They were four times stronger numerically, ten
times better equipped, a hundred times stronger in the
air. He exchanged a few words with the artillery commander he had just left. Whatever compulsion was
called for, those horses must be buried. The whole en-

trenched camp stank—the stench of modern war, foulness and corruption and high explosives. Here, where the dead had been buried, the shells of the Allies had horribly caused the earth to give up its dead. He must remember to give orders about that.

He stumbled through a filthy puddle. By his action today he had prolonged the defense by a few hours. The Allies would have to regroup and replenish with ammunition before they renewed their assault. If the counterattack had regained the crossroads he might have gained a day—two days, even. But it had failed, and there was not a single battalion—not even a battalion, as battalions were measured nowadays, with less than company strength—in reserve. Infantry, engineers and cooks were all in the front line. No; in a cellar in the village were two men under arrest. At headquarters they were waiting for him to confirm the court-martial sentences; he had postponed his decision until his return. Yet the sentences would have to be carried out. He had been remiss in even allowing that short delay. Prompt and inevitable punishment was necessary to keep the garrison fighting. Yet did it matter about two miserable men who had attempted to desert, when ten thousand men were going to die? Dexter shook his head, not in dissent but rather to shake off evil thoughts, as he plunged on.

Headquarters were in the church, in the crypt below the church, for of the building itself only a fragment of one wall still stood. The rest was piled about in jagged heaps of masonry. Dexter went in through the sandbagged and camouflaged entrance, down the stone steps, past the signalers in the outer dugout, and into the crypt, where four candles struggled to burn in the foul air, and the chairs and tables of the staff were ranged round the tomb of the saint. Gruppenfuehrer Frey, left in charge when the General went to Canal Corner, rose to greet him.

"Congratulations, General," he said, in his shrill voice, and the General stared at him in astonishment. There was nothing in the events of the past few hours—or days—or weeks—which called for congratulation. Frey turned back to take a little box from his improvised desk, opened it, and handed something to the General with an extravagant gesture; it was something metallic, which glittered, and lay cold in the General's hand.

"The Knight's Cross of the Iron Cross!" said Frey. "The Ritterkreuz! What a pleasure it is to hand it to you, General. It was never better deserved."

"How did this get here?" demanded Dexter.

"The plane—you didn't see it pass over? This morning—it dropped a message packet."

"I did not see it," said Dexter. Perhaps it had flown over while he had been rallying the Landeschuetzen Battalion at Oak Tree Corner. He had been too busy to notice the only German plane the garrison had seen since the siege began.

"Was there anything else in the message packet?" asked Dexter, sharply still.

Frey's fingers fluttered back to the desk.

"The letter from the Chief of the Military Cabinet enclosing the Ritterkreuz," he said. "A most flattering letter, General."

Dexter glanced through it. A flattering letter, certainly—nothing beyond flattery either. The Higher

Command, now that Germany was falling in ruins, avoided realities and confined its attention to trivialities like Knight's Crosses.

"Anything else?"

"Personal orders for me from SS Head Office."

In the fantastic disorder into which Germany had fallen it was possible—it was a certainty—that an SS officer should receive orders independently of his commanding officer. Dexter could not even ask what those orders said.

"Anything else?"

"Yes. A small amount of mail for some of the units of the garrison. I have not yet decided to distribute it. As Political Officer I have to consider—"

"Anything for me?"

"One letter, General."

Dexter knew what it was the instant he saw it. He snatched it from Frey's hand. Frey's fingers were twitching to open it, the born spy that he was; and as Political Officer with Himmler's authority behind him he could have demanded that it be shown him, but he knew that —at least in an isolated garrison like this—there was a practical limit to the power delegated to him. Dexter would not have allowed him to see Aloise's letter, not for anything on earth. Dexter stood holding it, yearning inexpressibly to open it and read it, but he would not do so in Frey's presence. When he could get a moment's privacy he would read it. It would afford him a brief glimpse of another world; it would be torment as well as unmeasured happiness, he knew. He would be reminded of Aloise's steadfast love for him, the comfort of it, the security of it, even while he was here, plunged deep into hell. Hell was all round him, and he would never escape from it; the letter he held in his hand would open a chink through which for one small moment he would be able to peer through into heaven.

Hell was all round him, demanding his attention.

"Have any reports come in?" he asked. He must attend to his duty before reading Aloise's letter.

Busse, the Assistant Chief of Staff, had them ready.

"Verbal reports, sir," he said, holding his notes of the telephone conversations in his hand. "Barmers says— perhaps I had better give you his exact words, sir."

"Very well," said Dexter. Barmers was the senior medical officer in the garrison.

"He says, 'It is my duty to report to the General that I can do nothing for the wounded that are coming in. Anesthetics and dressings are completely at an end, and plasma nearly so. The regimental aid stations are asking for morphine, and I have none to give them. The newly wounded must lie in the open outside the hospital to wait their turn for operative treatment without anesthesia, and that will not be until tomorrow morning. I should not really have spared the time to make this report.' That is the end of the report, sir."

"Thank you," said Dexter.

"The adjutant of the 507th Artillery Regiment reports—"

"I saw him on my way back. I know what his report says."

Ten rounds left per gun, and very few guns serviceable.

"General Fussel asks for the return of his Ost Battalion."

Fussel commanded the 816th Division on the far side of the perimeter. His division had been stripped of every available man to make the counterattack.

"I left that decision to you, sir," interposed Frey.

"The Ost Battalion must stay where it is," decided Dexter.

"Fussel has no reserves at all, sir," said Busse, in gentle warning.

"I know that. Anything else?"

"The assistant quartermaster general—"

"I can guess what he has to say," said Dexter, looking round at the gloomy face of Becker, the officer mentioned. "Anything else?"

"The court-martial findings, sir."

"Yes," said Dexter.

Two men waiting to be shot, two men who had been detected in the act of desertion. There could be no mercy for them if the garrison were to be held together. The sooner they were shot the stronger the effect on the others. It was his duty not to delay. And yet— He had fought a good fight. His iron will had implemented his immense tactical experience. Under his leadership his garrison had beaten off two assaults and had at least temporarily checked the third. In the hands of a bungler the defense might well have collapsed on the third day, and now it was the seventeenth. Surely he was entitled to some reward for that, something more satisfying although less tangible than the Ritterkreuz? He could spare two lives. Or could he even spare ten thousand? He was suddenly aware that Frey's eyes were fixed on his face, and he hoped that his expression had revealed none of his feelings.

The squawk of the telephone came as a fortunate diversion. Any call through to the central command post must be important, as only half a dozen officers had the right of direct access; routine calls were dealt with by the staff officer in the outer room. Frey picked up the telephone, as was his natural duty as Chief of Staff, but Dexter bitterly attributed to him a greedy inquisitiveness even in this hour of disaster.

"Chief of Staff," said Frey. "Yes. I hear. Yes. Yes."

He looked over at Dexter, the telephone still in his hand.

"Fussel," he said. "He thinks he can hear armor moving up behind the embankment at La Haye. Coordinates—"

"I know the place," said Dexter. "Tell him it makes no difference to his orders."

Fussel apparently expostulated at the far end of the wire; there was a brief argument before Frey put down the telephone again. Well might Fussel expostulate, too. If the Allies were bringing up tanks they could burst through Fussel's sector as if it were a paper hoop. So far the garrison had seen none.

"It may be only a ruse," said Busse.

That was possible. There were plenty of ways in which the Allies might simulate the sound of tanks advancing in the shelter of the embankment. Dexter could not believe that it was only a ruse, all the same. Nor could Frey, obviously. There was a pinched look about his thin face as he stood, still fingering the telephone. But when he raised his head and met Dexter's eyes again the pinched look was transmuted into something more vicious. Ratlike, perhaps. Frey was a cornered rat facing finality with bared teeth. He drew attention with a gesture to the letter still unopened in Dexter's hand.

"I *hope* the Baroness is well," he said, his shrill voice shriller even than usual with the heightened tension. "I *hope* she is well."

There was a hysterical edge to the remark; in other circumstances the words might have been utterly casual, but now there could be no doubt about their implication. Frey was using a threat to insure the death of ten thousand men. He was infected with the same madness that was being displayed by the whole Party from the Fuehrer downward, with the same insane lust for destruction. If the Party were doomed to perish then nothing German was to survive. The men could die, the women and children starve, the whole area of the Reich was to be left a depopulated desert in the final Götterdämmerung, without one stone left upon another in its silent villages and cities; that was the only way left for the Party to assert itself, and those stony deserts the only memorial the Fuehrer could now hope for. Frey, for his own part, was insuring for himself, like some petty Attila, the company of ten thousand spirits of men when he himself should pass on to whatever he thought lay beyond the grave. That was why he was reminding Dexter about the letter, about Aloise.

Dexter's pistol was at his belt, and he was actually tempted at that moment to draw it and to kill this madman. But that would be no help to Aloise. It would not remove her from the power of the SS; rather would it— if the news reached Germany, as it might with so many informers about—rather would it insure the worst, the torture chamber, the pincers—the—the—Dexter felt his own sanity to be on the point of breaking down, and he mastered himself by a frightful effort. He wanted to shout and storm; the steadiness of his own voice when he spoke surprised him—it was as if someone else were speaking.

"I had forgotten my letter," he said.

Of a sudden he felt intensely weary. And he was cold, too; shuddering a little. That had to be controlled in case they thought he was trembling. Another determination was forming in his mind.

"I shall go and rest," he said. "For fifteen minutes."

Frey and Busse nodded, their eyes fixed on his face, and their gaze followed him as he walked slowly and heavily over the flagstones to the corner where a suspended blanket screened his bed. He remembered to take a candle with him, and once inside the screen he set it on the bracket at the head of the bed. He would need that much light to read his letter; even though he would need no light for what he was going to do after that. He turned back from the bracket to draw the screen close, and in that moment he saw Busse's face, tortured with pity. That was the last thing he saw before he drew the blanket.

Inside the screen there was only room for the bed. He had to lie down on it to read his letter. He ought to take off his boots. Otherwise he would smear the bed with mud, and the thought disturbed his orderly mind; he remembered the general orders he had issued to the garrison on his taking command, to the effect that every man who allowed himself to be unclean would be severely punished. That had been necessary to keep the garrison up to the mark, to maintain them as disciplined soldiers to the very end. But this was the very end, for him at least. And if the bed were soon to be fouled with blood and brains, a little mud hardly mattered. He lay down and swung his muddy boots up onto the bed.

His hand holding the letter lay on his breast, and there was a moment's incredible temptation not to read it. He was so weary. The deed he had in mind to do was an easy way out for him. It would be the end of his troubles. It might well save Aloise's life, too. A bloody sacrifice might appease the madmen of the SS. And even if it did not, he would know nothing about it. He would be at peace, even if Aloise—No; he must not think along those lines.

Nor would it solve the problems of the garrison. With his death Frey would take command, and the ten thousand men were still doomed. He must not think about that, either. As he could do nothing to save them he must congratulate himself on ending his own misery and he must give no further thought to theirs. That was cowardly. The horrible system that had mastered the Reich was forcing even Friedrich von Dexter into cowardice; could there be better proof of its inherent evil?

To draw his pistol he had to lay down the letter. As his hand touched the cold butt he withdrew it again. He must read Aloise's letter, of course. He would read it twice, and when for the second time he had read the last dear word he would draw the pistol, quickly. His mouth actually softened into something barely like a smile as he thought of Aloise's tenderness and love. He opened the letter.

My Dearest,

This letter brings you from your loving wife every good wish, wherever you may be, whatever may be happening, and with my good wishes my deepest love, which you know you have had during all the years of our marriage.

But, dearest, I am afraid that this letter is going to add to your unhappiness. I have bad news for you. I did not tell you about it when we were last together, because at that time you had too many troubles already and I could not add to them. I kept it a secret from you then, but now I have to tell you.

Dearest, I shall not be alive when you receive this letter. I have a cancer. Dr. Mohrenwitz has told me so, but I knew it before he told me. I made him tell me. And he told me that it is in the same place as Frau Engel had hers, and you remember what happened to her, dearest. It has not been too bad until now, but now I cannot go on. Dr. Mohrenwitz has been giving me pills to make me sleep and to ease the pain, and I have been saving them up. Tonight, after I have posted this letter, I am going to take them all at once. I have made all the arrangements and I know I shall die.

So, I have to say good-by to you, dearest. I have to thank you for every bit of happiness I have enjoyed during the last thirty years. You have always been the best, the kindest, the tenderest of husbands to me, and I have loved you with all my heart. And I have admired you as well—I have been such a fortunate woman to have a husband I could admire as well as love—your honesty and your sincerity and your thoughtfulness and your care.

I only wish I could have done more for you, dearest. I used to wish I could bear all your sorrow as well as my own when we lost our dear boys. But now you know that I have no more sorrow or unhappiness or pain and that while you read this letter I shall be at peace. Tonight I shall only be thinking of you, dearest, as I always have done. My last thoughts will be of you, always and ever my very dearest.

Good-by, darling. Good-by

Eternally your A.

That was the letter. Dexter read it twice, as he had planned, but not twice through from beginning to end as he had thought he would. He read it jerkily, going back to reread each line. It was hard to focus his eyes on the words; perhaps because the light of the single candle was so dim. But he finished the reading and lay still, the letter on his breast. He was conscious only of his dreadful sense of loss. A world that did not have Aloise in it was not the same world as he had lived in for all these years. It was not a world in which he wanted to live. He remembered why he had come in here. He put his hand down again on the butt of the pistol, and perhaps it was the cold contact that recalled him to other realities. Aloise was dead—was dead—was dead. She had said she would have no more sorrow or unhappiness or pain. She had not said that now she would be beyond the power of the SS, but that was equally true. Dexter stiffened, as he realized that he still had a duty to do, a duty which he could now carry out.

The realization held him rigid for some seconds as he thought about the situation, and then he relaxed as his numbness vanished and his thoughts began to flow freely again. He was a man of action, bred and trained to make rapid decisions, and born with the firmness of will to execute them. There was no time to waste. He must act, and he burst instantly into harsh action. He drew his pistol as he swung his legs off the bed; he released the safety catch as he stood up. With his left hand he held aside the screening blanket, and he emerged into the crypt with his pistol pointed and ready.

They were all three of them still there. Frey and Busse and Becker; they were waiting to hear the pistol shot behind the screen, and they looked round in surprise as Dexter came bursting out. Dexter pointed the pistol at Frey, who was the dangerous man—he could trust the other two.

"Move and you're dead!" said Dexter, his lips hardly parting sufficiently to allow the words to escape him.

"But—but—" began Frey, backing away in astonishment from the weapon.

"Stand still! Put your hands on your head!"

Perhaps some unconscious memory of the American Western films that he had seen long ago, in the days of the Weimar Republic, prompted Dexter to give that order, but he had seen long lines of Russian prisoners emerging from strong points after surrender, with their hands on their heads too. Frey obeyed; no sound came from his lips although they moved.

"Busse!" snapped Dexter.

"Sir!"

"Telephone to Fussel. Get through to him at once."

"Yes, sir," said Busse, advancing to the telephone.

"You're going to surrender!" said Frey, finding his shrill voice again, his body jerking with emotion while he could not gesticulate, hands on head.

"Yes," said Dexter.

He was going to save ten thousand lives for the Germany of the future.

"But your wife!" said Frey. "Remember—"

"My wife is dead."

"But *my* wife—my children—"

Frey's voice went higher still, into a scream. It all happened in a second. Frey's excitement completely overcame him, and he put his hand down to his pistol. But to draw the weapon took far too long. Western films had not taught Frey to be quick on the draw. Before he even had the holster unfastened Dexter shot him twice, the reports resounding like cannon shots in the restricted space of the crypt, and Frey fell dying on the tomb of the saint.

"That's better," said Dexter. "Now I can speak to Fussel myself."

That night the B.B.C. broadcast the news of the surrender of Montavril. In five languages the news was broadcast over Europe. Ten thousand men came out from the shadow of imminent death into the prisoner-of-war camps of the Allies. All through the night Allied doctors toiled over the German wounded. Far away in East Prussia, in a gloomy headquarters dugout deep below the gloomy pine woods, a frantic tyrant raved like a maniac—like the maniac that by now he was—because ten thousand men were alive whom he wished dead.

That night four men knocked at the door of a house in the Welfenstrasse. A dignified old lady opened the door to them, and at a glance recognized their uniforms.

"I was expecting you gentlemen," she said. "You want me to come with you?"

"Come," said one of the four.

The old lady's hat and coat hung in the hall ready at hand, and she put them on quickly, and walked out with the men to the waiting car. She was still alive, and she showed no signs of the cancer she had said she had. But as she had promised, her last thoughts were of the husband to whom she had written.

TO BE GIVEN TO GOD

The expression "deodand" has been absent from English law for more than a century, although it is still to be found, very rarely, in the legal codes of some of the States of the Union. It is an Anglicization of the Latin *Deo dandum*, "to be given to God," and from the early Middle Ages until last century the idea of the deodand played a most important part in the development of English law. The deodand was the object that caused the death of a human being, and it was itself, in the minds of the people of the dark ages, tainted with homicidal guilt; it was something to be set apart, looked at askance, and devoted if possible to charitable uses. When inquiry came to be made into the causes of violent death, when the coroner was developing his functions and jurors theirs, the question of which particular instrument occasioned the death was a matter of importance. It assumed an importance economic as well as moral when the person responsible for the administration of justice—the lord of the manor, the sheriff, the bishop, or the king—discovered that deodands might constitute a useful source of revenue. Sometimes the deodand might be worthless, as for instance if a man were killed by a well-thrown rock, but if on the other hand a farmer was run over and killed by his own wagon and horses the deodand might be valuable, and of great importance to a needy king who early found that the allocation to charity of the proceeds of the sale of a deodand was not too carefully inquired into, once the deodand had been confiscated.

So that the identification and valuation of the deodand were matters to be strictly attended to, and the student of law very early finds indictments charging, for instance, that A.B. did feloniously and with malice aforethought kill one C.D. by stabbing him with a knife value one shilling; in fact in many trials the court would be found devoting more attention to the value of the deodand than to the guilt of the accused. By the middle of the nineteenth century superstition had declined to such a point that a sweeping act of parliament was able to put an end to the whole business, even though there still lingers among many people and peoples a special interest in the instrument of death, whether it be the hangman's rope or the assassin's pistol which is exhibited in a chamber of horrors. But the deodand has disappeared from English law, and its very name has almost vanished from the dictionary. It is kept there only by the fact, already stated, that any study of the history of English criminal law can be complete only if it includes consideration of the deodand.

In 1945 a trial of war criminals was being held before a British Military Court in Germany. The accused sat in two long rows in the dock, so many of them that for convenience of identification by witnesses they wore large distinguishing number cards on their chests. The trial had opened some days earlier; the accused had listened to the indictment, read out both in English and in German, to the effect that they, as members of the staff of Rosenberg concentration camp, and responsible for the well-being of persons interned there, had, in violation of the law and usages of war, been concerned in the deaths of various persons, some of whom were named in the indictment. The indictment, in its strictly moderate wording, made no attempt to enumerate all the hundred thousand people who had died in Rosenberg concentration camp, nor, when it went on to charge the accused with "causing physical suffering" did it hint at the unspeakable horrors which had been of daily occurrence there.

But the speeches of the prosecution, even though, in accordance with the best English legal tradition, they were worded with considerable restraint, told of many of these things, and the evidence of innumerable witnesses had confirmed what counsel had put forward. Day after day battered wrecks of humanity had appeared in the witness box to tell stories of gas chambers, of beatings and killings, of starvation and disease, of torture and murder. Day after day, when asked to identify the persons responsible, the witnesses had turned towards the dock and had given the identification numbers of various of the accused. Most frequently of all had they spoken about Number Seven.

For the man who wore that number was named in the indictment as Peter Schiller; until the end of the war he had been Sturmbannfuehrer Schiller, the commandant of the camp. There was nothing exceptional about his appearance. His gray eyes were slightly protuberant; his close-cropped fair hair was receding rapidly from his forehead. There was perhaps a slight heaviness about his jowls, but that might well be indication of mild stupidity rather than of ferocity—he was, in fact, a rather stupid man. He had listened to the trial with a good deal of bewilderment. His processes of mental readjustment were slow, and even now he found it hard to believe that the statements made by the human cattle in the witness box could possibly be harmful to Sturmbannfuehrer Schiller. Six months ago no one in all Germany would have listened to a word they said, or would have paid the slightest attention to any complaint they might make, if some extraordinary circumstance had given them the chance to complain. Schiller's conscience was absolutely clear. He had done nothing whatever that a man could be ashamed of, and it was with a mild contempt that he listened to the evidence; nor could he really understand why his counsel, the learned Dr. Meier, should trouble to cross-examine them. Meier had been indefatigable during the trial, popping up and down at every possible opportunity, interposing questions, making suggestions; occasionally he had even put forward ludicrous theories, to the effect for example that Schiller had been away on leave at the time of some particular occurrence. It was all faintly absurd, and in Schiller's mind Meier was absurd, too, for all the dignity of his black court gown. No one would have paid much attention to Meier, either, six months ago—just a wordy old lawyer whose activities then could only be aimed at hindering the prompt administration of the affairs of the Third Reich. The conferences he had had with Meier, in the little room at the back of the court, had been faintly irritating as a result of Meier's misplaced earnestness and anxiety. Schiller had no doubt at all about the fact of his own innocence, nor did he doubt that to a court of gentlemen, a court of men whose trim uniforms and rows of medal ribbons proved that they were dedicated to the service of the state, he would demonstrate it easily enough when the time came.

That time was now. His name was called—just "Peter Schiller," no "Sturmbannfuehrer"—and Meier looked over at him with a gesture. He rose and walked out of the dock to the witness box. He was entirely unconscious of the sensation he was causing, completely insensible to the atmosphere of the court. Even the British soldiers acting as guards in the court, standing stolidly at attention, were tense within themselves as Schiller walked the few steps across the court. This was the monster, the beast, the ravening man-eater whose jaws dripped human blood, who had presided at scenes of horror and cruelty surpassing anything recorded since the days of Attila. The ceremonial massacres in the kingdom of Dahomey, the sack of Magdeburg or of Badajoz, the holocaust in the burning theater in Chicago—nothing had ever equalled the agonies of Rosenberg Camp, and those slightly protuberant gray eyes had witnessed those agonies, and those slightly flabby lips had ordered them. Now that Hitler and Himmler were dead, now that the newspapers of the world had published descriptions of Rosenberg Camp, and the theaters had even shown films of it, Schiller was the best-hated man in the world. A dozen nations were clamoring for his life; hundreds of millions of people who had not heard his name three

months ago now thought of him with shuddering loathing, but he did not know it. He was as stupid, as im-
pervious, as only a man could be who had consented to
do the things he had done. He took the oath and stood
waiting; yesterday Meier had discussed this question of
the oath with him, pointing out that the rules of the
court gave him the choice either of making an unsworn
statement from the dock on which he could not be
cross-examined, or of giving sworn evidence from the
witness box where he would have to submit to questioning by the prosecution. He had chosen without hesitation to make a sworn statement, for he feared no
questioning, he had nothing whatever to conceal, and
he even cherished a few grievances regarding his own
treatment which he wished to air—this court of gentlemen would listen to them, he was sure, and would
probably administer a public rebuke to the uneducated
people who had handcuffed him and had treated him
with even worse contumely than that.

Meier was standing before him, dignified in his black
gown and wearing an odd expression of misplaced pity
and anxiety on his thin sensitive face.

"Tell us about the conditions in which you joined the
SS," said Meier gently.

Sentence by sentence, led skillfully by Meier's questions, Schiller told his story, even though parts of it were
a little irksome to relate publicly. Of his leaving high
school, of his search for employment in a disordered
world where skilled and unskilled alike stood in lines
waiting hopelessly for work—and even hopelessly for
bread. Schiller did not want to tell of those days as an
unemployed hobbledehoy; they did not accord with his

later power and dignity and security, but Meier had
been so urgent during their early discussions that he had
agreed to suffer the indignity. He was glad when his
story reached the point where he enlisted in the SS (he
did not lay any stress on the unwonted food and warm
clothing and pocket money his enlistment brought him)
and he could go on to describe the recognition he received and the promotion that followed that recognition.
He had worked industriously, obeying orders to the letter, never tiring, never faltering. The authorities had
clearly looked on him with an approving eye and he
had been promoted steadily from the lowest rank of all,
from simple SS-Mann to Rottenfuehrer and then to
Scharfuehrer; he had crossed the difficult hurdle to Untersturmfuehrer, and five years back he had been promoted to Sturmbannfuehrer; no mean achievement for
a friendless and not very well educated man.

As the interpreter droned on translating his statements Schiller felt his pride and self-confidence—a little
shaken by the recollection of the hateful memories of
adolescence—welling up within him again.

"You were always acting under the orders of superior
authority?" asked Meier.

"Of course," answered Schiller; some of the questions
Meier was asking him were quite puerile.

"You never doubted for a moment that those orders
were legal?"

"Legal?" echoed Schiller, quite puzzled.

His reply was drawn from him so quickly that the interpreter had had no time to translate Meier's question,
and while that was being done Schiller had a moment
to contemplate the ridiculous implications of the ques-

tion. How could orders from above be anything other than legal? How could the possibility be even contemplated that he could question their legality? The sort of people he took charge of under those orders might question their legality, but he was not that sort of unstable person.

"You were aware that the Enabling Law conferred on the Chancellor of the German Reich, Adolf Hitler, gave him full powers to do whatever he thought fit, and to delegate his authority as necessary?"

The Enabling Law?

"I'd heard of it," said Schiller, somewhat vaguely.

At the time when the Enabling Law was passed by the Reichstag he had been busy—that was the time of the great flood of arrests—but he spoke nothing but the truth when he said he had heard of it. He had been much preoccupied with the business of cracking the heads of liberal deputies and trades union leaders, and with throwing their senseless owners into prison vans, while the Enabling Law was being passed, and he had not troubled to think about the law's constitutional implications.

Meier did his best not to wince at Schiller's offhand attitude towards the Enabling Law, but he had to take the risk of pressing the point, for this was the vital moment of the defense.

"So that any instructions you received from the State Security Office were bound to be legal?" prompted Meier.

"Legal? Oh yes, of course."

"You would, in fact, have been breaking the law yourself if you had disobeyed your instructions?"

"Yes—yes, naturally."

To Schiller's mind it was proof of the fantastic orientation of Meier's ideas that the latter should labor this point of the legality of his actions. There were other aspects of the situation far more important; firstly that his orders came from above, through regular channels, and therefore had to be obeyed; secondly that orders were only questioned by the type of person for whom he had nothing but contempt, and thirdly—and truly not so very important—that in the inconceivable case of his not obeying his orders he would have had some very unpleasant things done to him.

Meier sighed with relief at having made his point clear with no greater damage to the defense, and passed on for a while to more indifferent subjects, coaxing helpful answers from his difficult client. But soon he had to ask about matters much more ticklish again.

"These prisoners who came under your charge—you had no personal animosity against them?"

"Why no, of course not," answered Schiller, quite astonished. It was the best answer he had made as yet.

When the farm laborer is sent out to clear a field of weeds he feels no personal animosity against those weeds; if a shepherd is entrusted with the duty of selecting from the flock in his charge those for breeding and those for slaughter, he does not feel any personal animosity towards any of them. Of course not. And similarly the laborer and the shepherd would not give a moment's thought to the feelings of the weeds or of the sheep—but Meier did not want to make that point.

"When provisions ran short and conditions became

bad in the camp you made representations to your superiors?" asked Meier.

"Yes," said Schiller truthfully.

He had been in two minds about it at the time; he had wondered whether he really should trouble Head Office with the news that his prisoners were dying of hunger at a time when Head Office had many urgent problems occupying their attention; incidentally he had wondered whether the fact of raising these difficulties would tell against his subsequent professional advancement, but he had decided in the end to make those representations.

"And in reply you received assurance that steps would be taken to remedy the state of affairs?"

"Yes," said Schiller. "But they never were."

Germany was in a bad way by then, with Allied bombers disrupting communications in every direction, with Allied advances necessitating the hurried transference and retransference of hundreds of thousands of prisoners from hundreds of prison camps. The promised increase of supplies never materialized, while the number of prisoners in his charge went on rising; overcrowding, disease, starvation to the point of actual cannibalism were what he had had to contend with. Soon he did not have enough sturdy prisoners or sufficient facilities to be able to dispose of the increasing daily number of dead. These people in the court would understand that.

Meier finished his questioning now, and with a bow to the members of the court returned to his chair. The British Major responsible for the prosecution was rising now. His uniform was of excellent cut, and he wore a treble row of ribbons on his left breast. He spoke German with an exactitude and a painstaking correctness that hinted at much conscientious labor in past years; his accent was indefinable, not Bavarian or Prussian or Austrian or Hanoverian, and it was this absence of character which really revealed that German was a language he had learned and had not acquired in childhood. He spoke German habitually in court, waiting for the interpreter to translate into English.

"These appeals you made to Head Office for increased supplies," he began, "is there any proof that you made them?"

"I have said that I made them," answered Schiller.

"None?"

"Under orders from Head Office before the surrender I destroyed all the camp records," explained Schiller. "And I believe Head Office did the same."

"Unfortunate, to say the least," said the Major. "But I suppose the Head Office had a great deal they wished to hide?"

That was unfair, thought Schiller.

"They did not wish to reveal any military secrets," he said.

"Military secrets? The Security Police had military secrets in their possession? Of any value a week before the end of the war?"

This certainly was unfair.

"It was our duty to do all we could until the surrender," Schiller asserted.

"You had no fear for your own skin if certain facts could be proved after the end of the war?" asked the Major.

"No. Of course not," said Schiller, with quite disconcerting lack of equivocation.

"You did not think that the Allied forces would be horrified when they found your camp full of dead and dying?"

"No," said Schiller, again quite genuinely. It was the fortune of war, it was the result of the imminence of defeat, that that had happened like that.

"The attitude of the British troops when they arrived at the camp surprised you?"

"Yes, it did."

Schiller had been utterly astonished by the behavior of the British officer who had searched the camp at the head of an advance patrol. He had whipped out a pistol and had kept it pointed at Schiller's stomach. He had spluttered and choked, his features writhing with nausea. Instead of receiving Schiller's surrender politely, as one gentleman should behave towards another whom he is meeting for the first time, he had had him seized, he had forced him and his guards at bayonet point to conduct them round the camp.

"You could not understand why you were arrested?"

"No. It was in violation of the laws of war."

Schiller was airing now the grievance he had cherished since that moment. Even his obtuse and unsympathetic nature was aware of the sensation his reply created when it was translated to the court, and he was glad. That ungentlemanly officer would perhaps meet with his deserts now.

"They maltreated us," added Schiller. More than one of the SS guards had received an inch of bayonet in his flesh for showing any resistance during that conducted tour. He himself had been rudely shoved about. The British soldiers had fingered the triggers of their rifles, would have shot Schiller and his guards then and there if they had been given the least excuse. Schiller had been acutely aware of that when they reached the women's compound and the Tommies had seen the ground carpeted with dying women and children.

"We will leave that question of maltreatment," said the Major. "Now that you have registered your protest. But tell me, were you and your staff sufficiently well fed during the last weeks of the war?"

"We had our rations," answered Schiller.

"You did not share them with your prisoners?"

"No," said Schiller. He could not have ventured to ask his men, the cream of the people on earth, to go short of food to supply the useless mouths of the prisoners. But he had the sense to be aware of the trend of the question, and he amplified his reply. "There were so many prisoners, and we were so few. One guard to two or three hundred prisoners towards the end—it would have been useless to share."

"And your duties had not deprived you of your appetite?"

"No."

"There were German troops in your neighborhood. Depots. Barracks. Did you not apply to them to help you out?"

"No."

Schiller could only answer with that monosyllable. It would have been a hopeless task to explain the whole situation to this stupid major. He would never realize that no army officer would lift a finger to help an SS

officer out of trouble—at least, not unless all the facts
were explained to him.

"Do you think they would have helped you if you had
asked?"

"I was bound by my oath not to reveal anything that
happened in prison camps," said Schiller.

"So you allowed people to die. How many?"

"All the records have been lost."

"Help us with an estimate. Ten thousand?"

"Perhaps."

"Twenty thousand?"

"Perhaps."

"Thirty thousand?"

"Really, I cannot say."

It was all most unfair. The Major had no understanding at all. Now he was going on with other questions
about things that had happened in the camp years ago.
Questions about what he called "brutality"; pointless
questions. Prisoners had to be guarded, they had to be
kept under control, they had to be selected for this and
for that in accordance with the orders from above. He
himself had been a very busy man; he had not been able
to supervise every detail of management, and it was in
accordance with the best principles of the service that a
free hand should be left to subordinates whenever possible. Probably there had been rough treatment; it was
only to be expected. There were never quite enough
guards and only an iron hand could maintain discipline.
And in any case what did it matter? Did it matter if the
cow on her way to market should receive a whack or two
from a stick to urge her on her way? Did it matter what
had happened to the creatures under his charge? Es-

pecially if the fate to which they were inevitably destined
were to be taken into account?

But Schiller had just sufficient tact to realize, after a
few questions, that it was a dangerous thing to be frank
about the matter. Allowance must be made for absurd
British prejudices; it was impossible to speak as one
realist to another. Schiller fenced cautiously after a
while. No, he did not remember such and such an incident. The witness's account was probably exaggerated.
Such and such may have happened without his knowledge, but he did not think it likely. No, he was not present when this other thing happened, whatever the
witness said. Schiller was pleased with his performance
by the time the Major sat down.

Now it was the turn of the various counsel for the
other prisoners. They rose one after the other with questions for him; each counsel was only concerned in proving the innocence of his particular client, and the matter
of Schiller's guilt or innocence was only of importance
to them as far as it affected the cases of their own
clients. The questions rained down on Schiller. Was such
and such an SS man present on such and such an occasion? What were the terms of his orders to so and so?
Could he not remember giving the Hauptscharfuehrer
charge of such and such a Kommando? The trend of the
questions was obvious; each counsel was anxious to
prove that his client was on leave, or was sick, or was
detached on some other duty at the time of some incident already attested to by previous witnesses, and if
that were clearly impossible, then they wanted Schiller to
say that it was by his orders that the thing was done, even
if that meant that Schiller would be incriminating him-

self. To the spectators, the press reporters, sitting in the enclosure reserved for the public, it was a horrible spectacle. The occupants of the sleigh pursued by wolves were struggling with each other in a wild melee, each man—and woman—trying to throw someone else out, no matter who or why, as long as he or she succeeded in remaining safe.

At last the questioning stopped, and now it was the turn of the President of the Court. He only asked two questions. Although he spoke in English, Schiller was aware from his tone, even before the questions were translated, of the quiet and impersonal attitude of the President of the Court. It was reassuring in the extreme. No one who heard the President speak could doubt for a moment that he was concerned only with ascertaining the truth. Schiller felt the fears and doubts which had begun to assail him during his cross-examination fall away again into insignificance. It must be quite clear to a gentleman of this sort that a true servant of the Reich, a man bound by oaths and owing allegiance to superior authority, could have acted in no other way than Schiller had acted; nor could the President with his Olympian calm give anything more than a passing thought—even if that—regarding what had happened to a few thousand individuals of inferior races.

Schiller answered the President's questions without reserve, glad of this opportunity of stating his position, man to man. Yes, the normal scale of rations allotted to his prisoners, before the chance shortages caused by defeat, was below the minimum scale allotted to any free civilian; about two thirds of the minimum scale, in fact. Yes, the orders which came down from Head Office regarding the gassing of batches of prisoners were always couched in a regular form, which did not include any reason stated.

There was a moment's pause now, and then Meier caught Schiller's eye and with a gesture indicated that he was free now to walk back to the dock. He returned to his place with his head held high, with no concern for the shameful and degrading number dangling from his chest. Meier was a fool—why should he wear on his stupid face that anxious and pitying look? And these others around him in the dock with their white faces and their trembling lips—they were weaklings frightened by bogies. Schiller sat on through the rest of the proceedings without paying too much attention. Meier made a long speech directed at the court. Probably it was good sense, all about delegated responsibility and international morality, but it all seemed very unnecessary. And then of course the other counsels had to say their various says, too. Silly little pettifogging lawyers attracting attention to themselves. And now the Major was on his feet again, trying to rebuild a case out of nothing. Schiller was glad when he sat down at last. There was still another long speech to sit through before the President uttered a couple of sentences in his dispassionate voice slowly translated by the interpreter. The court would now consider their verdict.

The ceremonial of the court came into action, like the slow easy motion of a well-oiled machine, guards and officers coming to attention, everyone filing out in prescribed order. Schiller went out along with the other accused, down the stairs where the sentries stood on guard, along the corridor to his solitary cell with the half door that allowed all he did to be observed from the outside. Well, it would not be long now. Soon he would cease to be "The Defendant Number Seven, Schiller" and would revert to his natural condition of an independent individual. He would be able to eat his dinner without having every mouthful watched by a guard—yet this was a good dinner, too; quite excellent, and he was hungry. After he had finished it he could lean back and doze in tranquillity of mind.

He was roused by the usual activity in the corridor, the stamp of military boots, the sharp utterance of military orders, and he rose to take his place in the line and file back into the courtroom. When at last they could sit, after the court had filed in too and seated themselves along the dais at the far end, a strange sudden silence fell upon the big room. The afternoon sunlight came in through the windows in diagonal bars. It was the silence of intense agonizing expectation. Schiller was aware that all round him his fellow prisoners were sitting braced and tense, some of them trembling. The President of the Court was sitting in his center chair on the dais, his arms resting on the table before him, his hands holding a long piece of paper. He began to read, speaking in his unknown language, in his calm dispassionate voice. Then he waited while the interpreter translated; the interpreter could never achieve that aloofness of intonation.

"Defendant Number One, Forster. The court find you guilty of the first charge and not guilty of the second charge."

There was a sharp exclamation along the row to

Schiller's left, a movement of precaution among the guards, and then Forster mastered himself.

The President was speaking again, while Schiller found himself filled with sudden disquiet. His self-confidence was ebbing out of him. That dispassionate voice did not sound to him any longer like the voice of common sense disdainful of vulgar foreign prejudices. Now it sounded like the voice of an arbitrary and unpredictable destiny, an immovable and inexorable destiny. The interpreter's voice followed.

"Defendant Number Two, Reinsch. The court find you guilty of all three charges."

Schiller leaned forward. His hands came together on his knees and clasped each other tightly. The voice went on. Defendant Number Three was guilty. Defendants Numbers Four and Five were not guilty; there were exclamations closer to Schiller now; Defendant Number Six was guilty, and Dorr beside Schiller—he had annoyed him all through the trial with his constant fidgeting and fretting—uttered a groan.

Still the President spoke. Schiller could not tell what he was saying. It seemed a long time before the interpreter translated.

"Defendant Number Seven, Schiller. The court find you guilty of all three charges."

So there it was. Schiller took a little time to realize all the implications, even though he had had that brief premonition. He did not hear the voices of the President and of the interpreter as they went on with the rest of the findings. He heard nothing, and he saw nothing. Emotions were rising within him; his heart was beating faster and faster. He knew a moment of fear. They might

sentence him to death; they might send him down the
same road as so many millions had been forced to travel
lately. Then he put that thought on one side. They could
not—they simply *could* not—do that to Peter Schiller.
That would be putting him on a level with the inferior
creatures whom he himself had dispatched, and that was
manifestly absurd. But they certainly might imprison
him, for years and more years. He might wear prison
clothes, be driven to forced labor by unfeeling guards,
he might never breathe free air again. That was a dreadful thought; the prospect was the more frightening because of the unquestioned power of life and death that
he had held for so long. Then it occurred to him that
the world was insane at the moment; these people had
allowed their prejudices to stultify their judgment. Later
on they would recover their good sense, re-establish a
proper standard of values, and would release him with
apologies. But it would be bad while it lasted.

At the same time that these thoughts were coursing
through his mind his emotions were growing more and
more intense, building up to greater pressures than could
have been thought possible. There was fear at first, but
soon the fear was forgotten, submerged under a wave of
resentment that seemed to roar in his ears. He was furi-
ously angry. He had led a steady, conscientious life, doing his duty, carrying out to the letter every order he had
received; he had been a superlatively good official, of
exactly the type necessary to set the world in proper order; he had been a good husband and father; he had
done nothing of which anyone might be ashamed. He
had never accepted a bribe, and God knew how many
had been offered him, bribes not merely of gold and of

flesh, but of sycophancy and adulation—never once had he allowed either self-interest or sentiment to divert him from the straight path he had visualized before him.

And he had been completely misunderstood. He had been insulted and threatened, treated with contempt and loathing. The hopes he had had of making his position clear and of receiving fitting apologies had been proved to be quite ridiculous. It was infuriating to be made ridiculous in his own eyes, to have it proved to himself that he had made such absurd errors of judgment. Mounting rage masked the momentary self-doubt. These stupid fools with their undeserved victory! His resentments, his consciousness of being misunderstood, his feeling that in a world gone wrong he was in the grip of forces unbelievably powerful and yet unbelievably blind, made him so angry that in the end there was room for no other emotion at all. There was hardly room for thought.

By that time the President had finished reading his long list, and the interpreter had finished translating. There was a slight bustle and stir in the dock. Someone —it was that fool Becker—came stumbling blindly past Schiller's knees. Those of the accused who had been found not guilty were being released from custody. They were going out to breathe free air. Schiller's rage took a new turn. This must all be the fault of that imbecile Meier. It had been his business to conduct Schiller's defense. He was a lawyer, one of that shifty and cunning breed; he was supposed to know all the tricks and turns of this legal nonsense. He must have bungled it. He must be utterly foolish—or worse—to have lost a case where his client's innocence was so clear cut and obvious.

Resentment against Meier built up Schiller's rage to higher pressures still.

Now the flat hateful voice of the President was being heard again, followed by the monotonous tone of the interpreter. The court would once more be cleared, to enable counsel to prepare pleas in mitigation of sentence. Two or three defending counsel rose to their feet with requests arising out of this announcement. Meier was among them. He was asking for something or other; Schiller had not been paying attention. But his request was granted, and the court entered once more into its old routine as it was cleared.

As Schiller stood waiting to file out he had a new thought. Pleas in mitigation of sentence! So all was not yet lost. Perhaps the business so far had been one more of the legal forms and ceremonies in which this strange people delighted. On account of some quirk of their silly law they had had to find him guilty, but now they were looking for some excuse to behave sensibly. It would be up to Meier to see that they were provided with one. He walked down the stairs to the corridor; a Tommy touched him on the arm and said something in unknown language, but the accompanying gesture made his meaning clear. Schiller was not to go into his cell to wait, but to proceed along the corridor to one of the rooms set aside for consultations between the accused and their counsel.

Meier was already there; he was setting down on the table the pile of law books he had been using for reference. Schiller strode in; his new hope had not greatly lessened his rage. Two soldiers entered behind him and took their position at attention beside the door; Meier

looked over at them and understood. Schiller had been
found guilty of charges whose penalty was death. From
now on he was to be under constant supervision lest he
should forestall the execution of justice.

"You don't seem to have done too well, Meier,"
snarled Schiller. "It's lucky you have this last chance of
setting things right."

Meier forced himself to meet Schiller's eyes, and was
astonished and tormented by what he read there. The
man did not know that he was inevitably doomed.

"I did all that it was possible to do," he answered. He
found with sick surprise that he had to exert self-control
not to allow his glance to wander away for one tiny moment towards Schiller's thick neck.

"Well, you must do better now," snapped Schiller.
"This nonsense has gone on long enough. Make sure
about this plea in mitigation of sentence."

It was not easy for Meier to decide what to do in face
of this utter misestimate of the situation. A few minutes
from now the court would be reconvened and Schiller
would be abruptly disillusioned. Meier still had a duty
towards his client, even though that client had been
found guilty, even though the sentence that would be
pronounced would be one that would within a few days
terminate all connection between counsel and client.
Schiller would be in the dock, with the eyes of all, the
eyes of the whole world, upon him. Would it be a kindness to leave him his last few minutes of illusionment?

There was the very grave danger that in that case
when Schiller heard the sentence he would behave in an
unguarded fashion. The possibility that there might be
some frightful scene in the dock—something which the

history books of next century might comment upon—
was appalling. If Schiller were to burst out in rage when
he heard his doom the world would have its impression
of him as a bloodthirsty savage only too well confirmed.
And if Schiller were to show the effects of shock they
would be interpreted as signs of fear, and that would
be worse. Neither in the immediate future nor during
the ages to come would it be well for the legend to de-
velop that the German who had sent so many to their
deaths feared death himself. It seemed the best thing to
do to warn him.

"What are you looking at me like that for?" demanded Schiller. "Haven't you thought about what you
are going to say?"

"It will make no difference whatever I say," answered
Meier.

"But—but I don't want to be sent to prison!"

"Prison? They won't be sending you to prison."

"Well—what *is* it? Can't you answer me? What do
you—what is—I don't understand."

Schiller's violence ebbed away. He slowly deflated under Meier's glance. Meier thought for a moment that
the sagging body would sag further until it would sink
to the floor, but then it braced itself up again, the head
was lifted and the shoulders pulled back. The stupid
face assumed an expression of wooden rigidity. There
was the faintest weakness, an almost imperceptible
shocked looseness about the lips, a quiver, of which
Schiller must have been conscious, for he forced his
mouth into a shocking macabre parody of a smile.

"You mean it will be death?" said the grinning lips;
there was a long interval after each word to show that

under the severity of the shock there was little strength left with which to think or speak.

"I am afraid so," said Meier, and then he added— for he saw the danger of misunderstanding even now— "I am quite sure of it. I am sorry."

This was dreadful; Meier even found himself listening expectantly for the bustle and orders outside that would indicate that the court was reconvening, so that the interview would come to an end. But there was no sign of that. He had to speak, to say something.

"Ever since the first day," he said "ever since the court rejected the plea of delegated responsibility, I knew it was hopeless. I knew that they would hang you. You don't understand how they hate you."

"Hate me?"

Was "hate" the right word? It really did nothing to express the feelings felt by a horrified world regarding the ex-Kommandant of Rosenberg. And Schiller knew nothing of it. What Meier was observing in his face was not only the fear of death but even more the realization that the world could hate him so much as to be determined to end the most valuable life in the world. It was understandable; even although during his imprisonment awaiting trial Schiller had been allowed newspapers to read he could not understand a word of English. The few German newspapers had naturally been cautious and reserved. Schiller was by no means the first man in history to be totally ignorant of the trend of public opinion towards himself. Now he was showing his ignorance again, as the toughness of his physical constitution reasserted itself along with his invincible stupidity.

"But they're all wrong!" said Schiller. "They don't understand! Can't you make them see?"

"I don't think it's possible," said Meier. He would not even say he would try again in his plea for mitigation. He dared not encourage false hopes; he was a lawyer who had passed his lifetime in courts, and even in the unaccustomed atmosphere of a British military court he could sense the inevitable.

"But you're a lawyer," said Schiller. "You ought to know. You've got all those books to study."

He pointed to the pile on the table with a violent gesture. Meier dreaded another outburst as Schiller's passion began to increase again. He could only fence for time.

"I've read every word in these books," he said, turning towards them.

Some were from his own library, some from public sources. One or two had been lent him by the British authorities; books in the German language about English law, written by German jurists. They had been hard to find—there had been a time when books about the liberty of the subject, and human rights under the Common Law, had been unacceptable to the authorities of the Reich, and most copies had been destroyed in bonfires.

"But they ought to tell you," said Schiller, with the touching faith of the unlettered man in the written word; a resurrected faith which had not been obvious in earlier years. He took up one of the largest books; there was a moment's doubt as to whether he would dash it to the ground or open it and slap at the pages. It was the latter that he did.

It was a ponderous volume, a typical monument of German research and erudition of the old days. *The Origins and Development of English Statutory Law from the Middle Ages to the Passing of the Bill of Rights,* by the most eminent German jurist of Bismarck's day. Schiller's feverish hands turned the pages.

"There must be *something*," said Schiller.

That book was written in the usual involved style employed by learned Germans; there were vast paragraphs whose meaning could only be ascertained by study. But the page on which Schiller's glance rested contained a word which Schiller knew well—"Death." He paused to read, for death was something very close to him. There was a strange word there, too, a foreign word he had never seen—"deodand"; he did not know that few enough English people were familiar with the word. The deodand, said the book, was the instrument of death. Whatever took a human life was for that reason forfeit. Public opinion demanded that the instrument should be given to God. No matter whether there was guilt or not, whether the killing were voluntary or involuntary, the instrument of death must be given to God.

Schiller started to read the paragraph again, clarifying his understanding of it, until it was quite clear. Guilt or no guilt, the instrument of death was forfeited to God, and these English still—so he understood—believed in God. The deduction was obvious even to his weary and harassed mind. There was at last an explanation for something that had appeared to be beyond explaining. Recent developments in German mythology helped him to his conclusion. He was to be sacrificed to the God of the English; that would account for everything, for the way in which they had ignored common sense, for what he had looked upon as sheer malevolence on their part, for the way in which they had brushed aside the most obvious appeals to simple reason.

"You don't know your own business," he sneered at Meier. "Here it is as clear as day."

Meier, utterly puzzled, approached to read the paragraph which gave the explanation, but at that moment sounds made themselves heard in the corridor outside the room. The court was reconvening. The lance corporal beside the door produced one of his few words of German.

"Komm," he said.

Schiller put the open book down on the table and walked steadily to the door. He was calm now; he was free of the uncertainties of ignorance. He could face his sentence unflinching. It would be hard to die, but not as hard as it would have been if he had been additionally tortured with the thought that a proper exposition of his motives would have saved him; he knew now that he was not misunderstood, or despised, or hated. He was to be given to the God of the English.

And—this was another point, one which had remained unexpressed, unformulated, but lurking in the background of Schiller's unclear mind for months like some nightmare monster—there was also the consideration that he dared not contemplate, that he could not possibly tolerate, the thought that he might be being justly condemned. He could not bear to think about what a monster he must be if that were the case. Rather than live with that thought it would be better to die, better to think of himself as a martyr to superstition.

THE WANDERING GENTILE

I don't know why this should have happened to me; the whole incident only occupied half an hour, and it might just as well never have taken place at all. I wish it had not. It was a month ago that it happened, when I was driving back to San Francisco after showing my prize collie Bessie. I had stopped for lunch at a roadside lunch counter, and was giving Bessie a final run before getting back into the car when they approached me for a hitch. They were a strange-looking couple—at least, the woman was ordinary enough, but the man was strange enough for two. He was old, bareheaded, with a shock of white hair that hung down sideways over one eyebrow. He dragged one foot, not so much with a limp as with a sort of hesitation. And there was a nervous tic in one side of his face, a twitching of the cheek, that was perhaps more marked at the moment because he was in a state of agitation. The woman was plainly looking after him, mothering him, perhaps, even though she was considerably his junior; not much past middle age, a faded blonde, gray haired now; you could guess that her eyes had once been of a brighter blue, just as you could guess that the clothes she was wearing had once been fashionable and expensive, but now they had lost their shape and so had she, leaving her plump and dumpy and badly dressed.

It was she who asked me for a hitch, in English marked by a strong foreign accent.

"The man we were with has stopped for lunch," she said, indicating with a gesture the car they had just quitted and the man pushing his way through the swinging doors.

"And don't you want lunch yourself?" I asked.

"No," she said. "We—we are in a hurry."

She spoke with a strong foreign accent, as I said. You must remember that fact when I record the conversation —the *w*'s were *v*'s and the *th*'s were complete failures. I hesitated, and while I did so the man barked something in a foreign language. I have said he was in a state of agitation; his fattish face, which might normally have been clay-colored, was flushed, and his gestures were jerky. The woman turned and spoke to him soothingly before addressing herself to me.

"He—he does not like to wait," she said.

"Where are you heading for?" I asked, and this time it was she who hesitated.

"It does not matter," she said, at last. "Where do you go?"

"San Francisco."

On Highway 101, going north from Los Angeles, San Francisco is the likeliest objective of all, so I was not re-vealing much by telling the truth, even if there had been any object in trying to conceal it.

"We would wish to go there too, please," she said at once.

The driver who is asked for a hitch usually has to estimate the chances of being held up or assaulted. But I had Bessie with me, and no man would lay a finger on me while Bessie was alive. Their only baggage was a shapeless bundle of moderate size.

"I'll take you," I said.

"Thank you," she said gratefully— What she really said, of course, was "Zank you."

"You can have the back seat," I said. "Here, Bessie."

It was the woman who opened the rear door and who handed the man in. Bessie came leaping into the car— she always does that as if she were going to a fire—and sat herself on the front seat beside me with her chin resting on the back so as to keep her eye on the strangers.

"All set back there?" I asked.

The woman shut the door.

"Yes, thank you."

So I started off up 101 again, and the woman began to talk rapidly to the man in the back seat.

Now with foreign languages I labor under a handicap that I believe is experienced by most people who have to employ them without being born linguists. When the need comes it takes me several minutes at least to adjust myself and to think in the new tongue—it is a serious inconvenience, often, because one first has to use the language at a moment when it is desirable to speak it well, when dealing with customs and passport officials on the frontier, and that is when I find my mind quite blank. Moreover, when at last I force myself to speak, it is the wrong language that makes its appearance; I find myself speaking halting French to Spaniards, or Italian to Frenchmen. Twenty years ago and more, during the time of the Weimar Republic, I spent a good deal of time in Germany, and I learned to speak German badly and to understand it comparatively well. Since that time I have had little occasion to use the language. During the gloomy months of 1938 and 1939 I would listen to Hitler's speeches on the radio, and occasionally since then I have attended showings of the *Blue Angel* and other German films, but that is all. So it was a minute or two before I could even be sure that it was German that the woman was speaking, and it was much longer than that before my ear became attuned sufficiently for me to understand even a part of what she was saying.

I heard the voices, and by shifting my position in the driver's seat I could get a glimpse of their faces in the mirror, or rather of the man's face, as he sat immediately behind me. He had lost his high flush, and his cheeks were now an unhealthy clay color, and he was sitting comparatively still. It was with surprise that I noticed what charming blue eyes he had—the deepest blue. Adonis eyes, fantastically out of place in that unhealthy face. I thought he must in his youth have been a man of mark. Then I realized he was speaking German, and I remembered the dragging leg and the twitching face; we all know what happened in the concentration camps in Germany. He must have been one of the few lucky ones who survived the horrible things that happened there (yet was he lucky to have survived?) and must have had the supreme good fortune of being admitted to the United States after the war.

"Have you been over here long?" I asked.

The German talk broke off abruptly.

"Not very long," said the woman after a pause—she had the same difficulty in changing from one language to another that I have.

"Do you like it here?" That is the inevitable question that every immigrant must hear hundreds of times.

"Yes, very much, thank you."

That is the inevitable answer that every immigrant makes. It brought the conversation to an end for the moment, and some seconds later the German talk recommenced, and I found that by now I could at least guess at the meaning of some of it.

"What did he say?" asked the man. His voice was harsh and toneless.

"He asked how long we had been here."

"Police?"

"No. No, my darling."

I caught the word *"liebe"* clearly, and "darling" is a fair enough translation. And the word *"polizei"* was unmistakable. People who have escaped from Hitler's Germany are obsessed with the thought of police.

"You are sure?"

"Yes, of course. Look at the pretty dog, darling." The woman said this to him in the same way that an adult would distract a child who had hurt himself.

"He is like Blondi," said the man—at least, I am nearly sure he said "Blondi." He extended his hand towards Bessie (of whose sex he was ignorant) as she rested her chin on the back of the seat, and Bessie gave the faintest of growls, deep in her throat.

"Now, Bessie," I said, and Bessie, like the well-trained show dog she is, submitted without further protest to a

caress from the trembling hand which patted her jaw.
But the man soon began to speak to his companion
again.

"He does not go fast," he said.

Normally I am a fast driver, but with some of my attention distracted towards my passengers I was certainly
driving slowly; other cars were overtaking fairly frequently.

"He goes fast enough," said the woman soothingly.
My ear was quite attuned to German now.

"And he goes to Washington?"

"Oh yes, my darling. He is going to Washington."

That made me stir a little in my seat. I had not said a
word about Washington, nor had she. I might have misunderstood, but it certainly sounded like "Washington"
pronounced as a German would pronounce the name;
and equally certainly neither of them said "San Francisco."

"It seems a very long way," said the man.

"Yes, it is a long way to Washington."

There was the name again, I was not mistaken. I could
not be.

"We have been traveling many days," said the man.

"Oh no, my darling. Not very long."

"It seems a long time," said the man. In the driving
mirror I could see him put a shaking hand to his forehead with a gesture of weary puzzlement.

"We shall soon be there," said the woman. She still
spoke to him as if he were a child.

"Of course it is a large country," said the man. "I was
forgetting. Washington is farther than Moscow."

"Yes, my darling, but we shall soon be there."

The situation was obvious to me now. The old man was a little touched in the head—as was likely to be the case with anyone who had escaped from Hitler's Germany—and was obsessed with the idea of going to Washington to lay his imaginary grievances before the Executive. His wife was keeping him from doing so, keeping him traveling round the United States, hitching, eternally hitching, always with the promise that they were on their way to Washington. I wondered how long she had been keeping this up; to the old man a month would appear no longer than a week. She was doing an intelligent thing, for although cranks in plenty arrive in Washington with grievances, violent ones are not long tolerated. An ill-timed outburst might result in deportation, if it did not end in the old man being put behind bars. My sympathy went out to her, to both of them, in fact.

"Are you sure you don't want any lunch?" I asked. "We can stop for a few minutes."

"Thank you. My husband, he does not like to wait."

"What does he say?" asked the old man in German, and the wife explained to him.

"Did you tell him who I am?" he went on.

"No, darling."

"Why not? He would join us."

"Oh no, darling."

I am only nearly sure that that is what he said. I cannot give you the German phrase he used—I caught it when he spoke, and understood it, but I cannot reproduce it.

"Another member for the Party," said the man, in a louder, more violent tone. "Perhaps—"

"No, darling. We have enough."

That word *Partei* was unmistakable. Everyone, even in pre-Hitler Germany, talked ceaselessly about parties.

"Yes. Thousands on thousands!" said the man. "The Day comes—"

"Hush, darling. Do not tire yourself now."

Der Tag—The Day; the Kaiser's Navy used to drink to that, and so did parties innumerable later on, Communists, Nazis, and all. As he spoke the old man had become wildly excited, half rising in the back seat and waving his arms. It took all his wife's persuasion and the touch of her hand on his arm to quiet him down. Bessie gave a warning growl.

"Quiet, old lady," I said, and then, over my shoulder, "Your husband must sit still."

"Yes—oh yes," said the wife, desperately anxious to please, and she whispered urgently to him. I was sorry that she whispered, because when the old man had asked if I knew who he was my curiosity was piqued. Presumably he had been the leader of some forgotten political party in pre-Hitler Germany, driven insane by the brutal treatment Hitler's political rivals met with on his accession to power. We drove on for some time in comparative quiet, the conversation in the back seat remaining at a low pitch, somewhat to my disappointment.

"You're Germans, I suppose?" I asked.

"Yes, we are Germans. Do you speak German, sir?"

"No" I said. That was half a lie, and I hesitate to admit it. But the temptation was overwhelming. Once more in the driving mirror I saw those handsome blue eyes turn towards the woman, and the brief conversation had to be translated to him.

"Ask him how long before we reach Washington," he said.

"How far do we have to go, sir?" she asked me; she was tactfully leaving the word "Washington" out of her question—I suppose it was a situation she had encountered plenty of times before.

"Three and a half hours, about," I answered, helping her out. That was the time it would take to reach San Francisco, but she told him three and a half days.

"There is time, then!" said the old man, excited once again. "Soon I shall be in the White House."

That confirmed what I was already sure of. He was as mad as a March hare, and heading for trouble. If he chose the White House as the place in which to air his grievances or speak about his theories he would not get beyond the second sentence.

"Yes, darling," said the woman. "Naturally."

I was curious to know who he was. He might have been someone prominent in pre-war German politics, perhaps even the leader of one of the innumerable German parties; in that case he would have undoubtedly gone into a concentration camp if he had been foolish enough to stay in the country after Hitler's accession to power, and that would account for his insanity—no other explanation was necessary.

"Did you have a bad time during the war?" I asked.

The woman waited, as usual, before answering.

"Yes, we had a bad time during the war," she said, eventually. The English she used was obviously modeled exactly on the English she heard spoken.

"What did he say?" asked the old man.

"He asked about the war."

"The war! Traitors! Cowards!" raved the old man—once more I had to guess at the meaning of the words he used, but I think I am right. My curiosity was still further aroused; I wondered to whom he was referring. Hitler and all his gang were traitors, without doubt, but it would be difficult to call them cowards. Presumably he meant some section of the opposition to Hitler. I shifted my position to look again in the driving mirror, and met his blue eyes looking at me. They glittered; that is the exact word. They had a kind of metallic sheen, like no eyes I had ever seen before, although I have seen something faintly like it in the glitter of the eyes of an excited stallion. They were fantastically out of place in that puffy, pasty face . . . Then we came to a town on the road, and I had to slow down for the twenty-five mile zone.

"We go very slowly," said the old man.

"We are going through a town," explained his wife as patiently as ever.

"We must go fast if we are to be in time to end the government," he replied.

That really made me stir in my seat; if he had revolution in mind, and not a mere public protest or a petitioning of the executive, he was heading for real trouble. And presumably he was a Communist, with this talk of overthrowing the government. And it occurred to me that when he had talked about arriving at the White House he had meant entering it as a conqueror, not as a visitor.

There was a good deal of local traffic in the town, and I had to shift gear and slow down to get through. At the traffic light there was a momentary stop, and during

that time (my attention for several minutes had been
fully taken up by the traffic) I heard plainly two words
in raucous German from the back seat—"International
Jewry!"; there could be no mistaking them, either. By
the time we had reached the end of the twenty-five mile
zone and I put my foot down to pick up speed the old
man was talking torrentially and explosively, so fast that
I could not follow what he was saying at all, especially
as there was still some slow-moving traffic to negotiate.
I could only devote the smallest part of my attention to
him. So that it was with a distracted mind that I heard
a word recur in his speech; he had said it before, and as
it had been quite meaningless to me I had paid it no
attention, accounting for it, I suppose, as some unimpor-
tant conjunction or ejaculation. But with its repetition I
began to hear it more plainly. It was the name of his
wife, Eva. Pronounced in the German way, "Ayffa," it
had quite failed until then to register in my mind. Eva!
It was something to know the woman's name, and there
was something more than that, too, but what it was I
could not think of for a moment. When I did at last
grasp the implications I put them aside as nonsense.
There must be at least a hundred thousand German
women called Eva. Besides, the Eva I thought of had
been dead for nearly eight years, a suicide.

The raucous voice behind me went on, always at the
highest pitch of emotion. Here and there I caught words
and phrases.

"Bolsheviks. I shall march in, Eva"—that name again
—"Plutocrats," "Jews."

"Yes, darling, yes," said Eva.

"Next week will be the hour!" said the old man.

A frantically gesticulating hand struck the roof of the car.

"Please calm yourself, darling," said Eva, soothingly as ever.

"Three days, did he say, Eva? Tell him to hurry."

"Yes, darling, I will ask him, but I cannot while you are speaking. Sit peacefully and rest yourself."

The high-pitched monotone died away, and I waited to hear how Eva would approach me. I felt embarrassed at this eavesdropping, but I admit I did nothing to end it.

"Will it be dark when we arrive, sir?" she asked.

"Very nearly," I answered, as evenly as I could. "It will be nearly five o'clock."

"Thank you, sir. You are very kind." She went on in German, "He says he is going as fast as is safe. Adolf."

It was then that I had the puncture. There was the short sharp hiss from the left rear wheel—just sufficient warning for me to slow down—and then the thump of the rim on the road surface. I drew onto the shoulder of the road and stopped.

"What is the matter?" demanded the old man in German.

"Why do we stop?" asked Eva in English.

"We have a puncture," I told her. "I shall have to change a wheel."

I opened the door and stepped down onto the shoulder of the road, Bessie hurrying after me. From the back seat came wild expostulations in German. I opened the rear door.

"I am afraid you and your husband had better get out while I change the wheel," I said.

Eva was patting Adolf's arm to quiet him, as I went round to the back to get out the jack from the rear locker. They climbed heavily out of the car, and stood in the late afternoon sunshine. Eva dragged the shapeless bundle out after them. Adolf was talking wildly again; I could hear him while I opened the locker.

"It should not happen," he said. "Do you remember how Wenck's army arrived too late at Berlin? Shall we be too late when we arrive in Washington?"

"No, darling, no," said Eva. "We shall be in time."

They were standing at the edge of the road by the car. The situation was plain to anyone driving by, and anyone could see in the late sunshine the white hair of the old man and the gray hair of his wife. It was likely that anyone would offer them a hitch even without being asked; I do not know if the woman signaled to the passing cars or not, but when next I looked up there was a Ford stopped beside them and they were preparing to get in. I saw Eva tenderly help Adolf to climb in, with his dragging leg and his twitching body, and I saw her hoist in the shapeless bundle and follow it herself. Then the car drove off, and I had not taken note of its number; at that time I had not made any decision at all about what I ought to do about the situation. My mind had not fully digested all this material, about Adolf with his harsh voice and his blue eyes, his hatred for International Jewry, his memory of a dog called Blondi, his Party, his excitability, his wife named Eva, his general named Wenck who had failed to relieve Berlin. He was a feeble old man, quite insane, in the charge of a motherly tactful woman who still loved him dearly.

It was not until I had changed the wheel and started

again up the road myself that I met a highway patrolman and flagged him down, and he looked at me pityingly when I told him that I was looking for a Ford sedan whose registration number I did not know and whose color I was not certain about. On U.S. Highway 101 there are plenty of Ford sedans. And then I told the patrolman who it was who was riding in the Ford, and he looked at me even more pityingly, but with a glance of sharp inquiry as well.

"That's who it looked like," I said hurriedly, making a clumsy joke out of it.

It was only because I was plainly sober that I was allowed to go on driving my car at all, and the patrolman stayed behind me until I reached the limit of his jurisdiction. And I have seen that pitying look on the faces of the one or two other people I have told about this incident, too. That is why I am telling this story as fiction. Pure fiction. Or perhaps that was not a man to whom I gave a hitch. It may have been a spirit, a wraith, doomed to eternal wandering.

FOR THE FIRST TIME IN PAPERBACK
—The **complete** story of the life and crimes of Adolf Eichmann, the most notorious criminal of our time

MINISTER OF DEATH
by QUENTIN REYNOLDS
F152, 50c

This book was begun several years ago by two Israeli journalists, Ephraim Katz and Zwy Aldouby, whose years of research —through personal interviews, through access to secret papers —gave them the most complete Eichmann file in existence.

Their material was gathered into book form by the brilliant author-journalist Quentin Reynolds, who made seven trips to Israel and worked on a 24-hour-a-day schedule to rush the facts into print.

"More intriguing than any detective story" **—New York Post**

"Fantastic and exciting...well told and authentically told by the authors who appear to have access to a mass of secret documents." **—The New York Times**

Eight pages of photographs, many of them exclusive

WRITE FOR YOUR COPY OF THIS DELL BOOK

Combat

EUROPEAN THEATER / World War II

Africa ... Anzio ... Omaha Beach ... Authoritative, on-the-spot accounts of the historic battle for Europe, some written by skilled war correspondents like Eric Sevareid and Alan Moorehead, others taken from the personal reports of the infantrymen who actually captured the ground, yard by incredible yard.

C107, 50c

Combat

PACIFIC THEATER / World War II

From the bombing of Pearl Harbor to the destruction of the Japanese fleet in Leyte Gulf, here is a full eye-witness account of the island war—unforgettably recorded by the soldiers, marines and correspondents who were there.   C108, 50c

Each volume complete with maps / running commentaries / introductions by an editor of YANK

Write for your copies of these outstanding volumes— Available only in Dell paperback